MACMILLAN READERS

INTERMEDIATE LEVEL

EMILY BRONTË

Wuthering Heights

Retold by F. H. Cornish

MACMILLAN

INTERMEDIATE LEVEL

Founding Editor: John Milne

The Macmillan Readers provide a choice of enjoyable reading materials for learners of English. The series is published at six levels – Starter, Beginner, Elementary, Pre-intermediate, Intermediate and Upper.

Level control

Information, structure and vocabulary are controlled to suit the students' ability at each level.

The number of words at each level:

Starter	about 300 basic words
Beginner	about 600 basic words
Elementary	about 1100 basic words
Pre-intermediate	about 1400 basic words
Intermediate	about 1600 basic words
Upper	about 2200 basic words

Vocabulary

Some difficult words and phrases in this book are important for understanding the story. Some of these words are explained in the story and some are shown in the pictures. From Pre-intermediate level upwards, words are marked with a number like this: ...[3]. These words are explained in the Glossary at the end of the book.

Contents

The People in This Story

WUTHERING HEIGHTS

Mr Earnshaw —— *m.* —— **Mrs Earnshaw**
d. October 1777 · *d.* spring 1773

Frances —— *m.* —— **Hindley** **Cathy** *m.*
b. October 1778 (1777) *b.* summer 1757 (Catherine) (spring
d. September 1784 *b.* summer 1765 1783)
d. 20 March 1784

Hareton —— *m.* —— **Catherine**
b. June 1778 (1 January *b.* 20 March 178
1803)

Joseph

4

THRUSHCROSS GRANGE

Mr Linton   *m.* —— **Mrs Linton**
d. autumn 1780   *d.* autumn 1780

Edgar   **Isabella** —— *m.* —— **Heathcliff**
b. 1762   *b.* late 1765   (January   *b.* 1764
d. September *1801*   *d.* summer 1797   1784)   *d.* May 1802

       m. —— **Linton**
(September 1801)   *b.* September 1784
              d. September 1801

Nelly Dean *b. 1758*   **Mr Lockwood**

5

PART ONE

1

Mr Heathcliff

Lockwood's diary

The year is 1801 and it is now the end of November. Two days ago I came to live in this old house – Thrushcross Grange. The countryside here in Yorkshire is beautiful – the most beautiful in England! There is a park[1] around the house, and beyond the park there are the moors[2]. I have come to this wild and lonely part of northern England because I want to be alone – away from everyone I know. The housekeeper here at Thrushcross Grange is a middle-aged woman called Nelly Dean. She looks after me well, but she is very quiet. So I shall have a peaceful time.

This is a lonely place and no one lives nearby. The village of Gimmerton is six miles away. I have rented[3] Thrushcross Grange for a year from my nearest neighbour, Mr Heathcliff. He lives four miles away. I have just returned from a visit to Mr Heathcliff. He is an unfriendly man who likes to be alone.

He was standing by a gate as I arrived at his house, early this afternoon.

'Are you Mr Heathcliff?' I asked.

He nodded his head, but did not speak to me.

'I'm Lockwood, your new tenant at Thrushcross Grange,' I said politely. 'I thought I should call on[4] you.'

He leant on the gate and stared at me. At last he said, 'Come in.' Then he turned and walked away from me towards the house.

I had thought that Mr Heathcliff would look like a farmer, but I was surprised. His clothes are made of fine cloth. He is a handsome man but he looks like a gypsy[5]. His eyes are dark and his hair is black.

Mr Heathcliff's house is called Wuthering Heights and it is not a comfortable house like Thrushcross Grange. The house is on the top of the moors where the weather is often very bad. There are strong winds and fierce storms so the house has been built with thick stone walls and very small, narrow windows. Above the front door, the date 1500 is carved into the stone. There is also a name – Hareton Earnshaw – cut into the stone. Perhaps Hareton Earnshaw was the first owner of the house.

I only saw one of the rooms inside the house. It had a stone floor, a large wooden table, a settle[6] and a few wooden chairs. And there were lots of dogs everywhere.

I decided that I liked my unfriendly landlord. But something unpleasant happened while I was at Wuthering Heights. Mr Heathcliff went out of the room to get some wine and I tried to make friends with one of the dogs. It immediately snapped and snarled at me. Then some of the other dogs attacked me too.

'You should never have left me alone with these dangerous dogs!' I cried to him as he came back into the room.

'Don't touch the dogs,' Mr Heathcliff said. 'They won't harm[7] you if you leave them alone.'

I tried to forget about what had happened and I continued our conversation. I think Mr Heathcliff is a gentleman[8] and an intelligent man, so I have decided to visit him again tomorrow. He was not very pleased when I said I would visit him again.

———

I have now decided that I do not understand my neighbour, Mr Heathcliff.

I visited Wuthering Heights again yesterday. It was a cold and misty afternoon when I left Thrushcross Grange after lunch to walk across the moors. I did not know that the moors are dangerous if the weather becomes bad.

The moors were bleak[9]. I saw no one. A bitterly cold wind was blowing. By the time I arrived at my neighbour's house, snow was falling and I was very, very cold. I knocked loudly on the door but no one came to let me in. I went round to the farmyard[10] at the back of the house and, at last, I found one of the servants in a barn. He spoke so strangely that it was difficult to understand what he said. But I did understand that he was a very rude, unpleasant old man.

'You'll find t'master behind t'barns[11],' he said. 'Go and find him if you want. He won't be pleased to see you. There's no one in t'house except t'missis. She won't let you in and I won't ask her to let you in.'

The snow was falling fast and I was angry now. I decided to go and knock loudly on the front door again. But suddenly a young man wearing dirty, untidy clothes came into the barn.

'You – come with me,' he said rudely. He took me into the house, to the room where I had been the day before.

There was a bright fire and there were plates and knives and forks on the table ready for a meal. Immediately I started to feel happier. Sitting near the fire was a young woman. She must be 't'missis' – Mr Heathcliff's wife – I thought.

She stared at me and said nothing.

'It's a very cold day,' I said politely.

The woman still said nothing.

I spoke again to her. 'I thought no one was in the house today,' I said. 'No one heard me knocking on the door.'

Then the young man spoke. 'Sit down – he'll be here soon.'

I sat down and there was silence.

The woman and the young man stared at me as if they hated me. Was the young man a servant or a relative of Mr Heathcliff? He was untidy and dirty, but he did not behave like a servant.

At last Mr Heathcliff arrived.

'Here I am,' I said cheerfully to him. 'I said I would visit you again. I will have to stay for a short time until it stops snowing.'

'It won't stop snowing today,' said my landlord. 'You were stupid to walk across the moors in this weather.'

'Oh. Could you ask someone to show me the way back to Thrushcross Grange?' I asked.

'No, I could not,' he replied.

Then he turned to the woman. 'Go and make the tea,' he said.

'Is he to have any tea?' she asked, pointing at me.

'Get the tea!' shouted Mr Heathcliff.

I now stopped believing that this savage, bad-tempered man was a gentleman. But I was polite to him. When the tea was ready and we were all sitting around the table, I spoke again.

'It must be difficult living in such a wild place,' I said to Mr Heathcliff. 'But you and your wife —'

'My wife is dead, sir,' he said.

He did not sound sad that his wife was dead.

'Oh!' I said, and I looked at the young woman.

'Mrs Heathcliff is my daughter-in-law,' said my landlord. He looked at her as if he hated her.

So she must be married to the young man who was sitting beside me, I thought. He was making loud noises as he drank his tea.

'I understand!' I said to the young man. 'This young lady is your wife.'

The young man's face went red with anger but he did not say anything.

'I said she was my daughter-in-law,' said Mr Heathcliff. 'She was married to my son.

'But,' he went on, 'this young man is certainly not my son. My son is dead.'

He did not sound sad that his son was dead.

'My name is Hareton Earnshaw,' the young man said to me.

9

It was very difficult to talk to these people. I went to look out of the window. The snow was falling very fast and it covered everything.

'How am I going to find my way home?' I asked.

But no one was listening to me. Mr Heathcliff and the young man left the room. Mrs Heathcliff started to take the plates off the table. The old man, Joseph, brought some food for the dogs.

He spoke roughly to Mrs Heathcliff. I realized[12] that Mrs Heathcliff and Joseph hated each other too. All the people who lived in this strange house hated each other.

'You're wicked like your mother,' said the old man to Mrs Heathcliff. 'You'll go to the devil like your mother.'

'Yes, yes, that's right,' replied the young woman. 'The devil will help me to make you ill.'

The old man moved backwards away from her. 'You're wicked! Wicked!' he said, as he left the room.

I tried again to get some help.

'Is there someone who can show me how to get back to Thrushcross Grange – a farmworker perhaps?' I asked.

'No,' she replied. 'There are no farmworkers – there's just Heathcliff and Hareton and Joseph and Zillah and me.'

'Then I will have to stay here tonight,' I said.

The young woman did not know what to say. 'I don't know. You'll have to ask Heathcliff,' she replied at last.

At that moment Heathcliff returned. I asked him if I could stay at Wuthering Heights for the night.

'There's no room for strangers here,' he said. 'You'll have to sleep in a bed with Joseph or Hareton if you want to stay.'

I did not want to sleep in a bed with either of them!

'I'll sleep on a chair in this room,' I said.

'You will not,' replied Heathcliff. 'I will not have a stranger walking around in my house while I am asleep.'

I was so angry that I left the house immediately. It was very dark and the snow covered everything. I walked around outside, looking for the gate out of the farmyard.

I was surprised when I heard Hareton speak from the door of the house. 'I'll go with him,' he said.

'No, you won't,' replied Heathcliff. 'You will go and feed the horses.'

'It is more important to look after a man than to look after the horses,' said the young woman.

'Keep quiet!' said Heathcliff savagely.

'When he dies on the moors,' she said, 'I hope his ghost comes back to haunt[13] you.'

Then I heard Joseph's voice behind me in the darkness. 'Oh, you're wicked, wicked! You'll go to the devil.'

I found Joseph in the barn with some cows. He had a small lantern and I quickly got hold of it. Then I made my way through the snow to the gate.

'I'll bring the lantern back tomorrow!' I shouted.

But Joseph called out to Heathcliff that I was stealing his lantern. Then the old man sent two dogs after me. They pulled me down onto the ground. The dogs would not let me stand up until Heathcliff and Hareton came to help me. Both men were laughing. My nose was bleeding and I was very angry, but I could not think of anything to say.

At last Zillah, the servant, came into the farmyard. She took me to the kitchen and gave me some brandy. Heathcliff stood and looked at me.

'Find him somewhere to sleep,' he said to Zillah.

2

Catherine Earnshaw

Later in the evening, Zillah took me upstairs to a small bedroom.

'Don't make any noise,' she said. 'My master doesn't like anyone to sleep in this bedroom. But this is the only bed in the house that no one uses.'

After she had left the room, I got into bed and looked around me. On the shelf where I had put my candle there was some writing. I could see it was a child's writing. The words were cut into the wood. There were many different sizes of letters. At first I thought that they all spelt the same name: Catherine Earnshaw. Then, when I looked more carefully, I saw that the name was sometimes Catherine Heathcliff and sometimes Catherine Linton. The writer did not know what she wanted to be called.

On the same shelf I found some old books. They all had Catherine Earnshaw's name in them. And she had written in them all. The girl had written about herself and her life.

Catherine's story was not a happy one. Catherine Earnshaw and someone called Heathcliff were friends. They walked on the moors, they played together and they spent all their time together. Was this Mr Heathcliff – my landlord?

Then, after Catherine's father died, her brother, Hindley, looked after her. He and his wife, Frances, disliked Heathcliff, and they kept Catherine away from him. They made Heathcliff into a servant. Catherine was very miserable. 'I never thought that Hindley would make me cry,' she wrote.

Joseph made Catherine and Heathcliff miserable too. Catherine wrote about a Sunday when Joseph made them read religious books for three hours. The children threw the books on the floor. Hindley was so angry that he sent the boy and girl to rooms in different parts of the house. But Catherine and Heathcliff escaped from the house and ran away to the moors for the rest of the day.

I started to feel sleepy and stopped reading Catherine Earnshaw's story. I soon fell asleep and started to dream. I dreamt that it was morning and that Joseph was going to show me the way home. But instead he took me to a church in the village of Gimmerton, near Wuthering Heights. I had to listen to the minister's sermon[14]. I dreamt that the sermon was very, very long and that I stood up and shouted at the minister. The minister was banging a long stick on the floor.

Then suddenly I was awake. There was a tree branch banging on the window. That was the banging I had heard in my dream.

Soon I was asleep and dreaming again. In my dream, I could still hear the tree branch banging on the window. In my dream, I sat up to open the window so I could stop the noise of the branch. The window would not open so I smashed my hand through the glass. I got hold of the branch to break it off. But, to my horror, it was not a branch. It was a small, cold hand.

'Let me in,' a child's voice cried.

'Who are you?' I asked.

I tried to take my hand away, but the child would not let go of it.

'I'm Catherine Linton. I've come home,' the voice said.

As the voice spoke, I saw the child's face through the broken window. I was terrified and the child would not let go of my hand. My terror made me cruel and I pulled the hand against the broken glass. Blood ran down onto the bed.

Again the voice cried, 'Let me in! Let me in!'

'I'll never let you in,' I cried. 'If you asked for twenty years, I would not let you in!'

'Twenty years...' the voice replied. 'I've been out here for

But . . . it was not a branch. It was a small, cold hand
'Let me in,' a child's voice cried. 'Let me in . . .'

twenty years.'

I was so terrified that I shouted out and woke myself up. I also woke my landlord who came running into the room.

'Dear God, Mr Lockwood!' shouted Heathcliff. 'What are you doing in here? Who let you sleep in this room?'

He was white with fear and he was trembling[15].

'Zillah brought me here!' I cried. I was still trembling after my terrible dream. 'She shouldn't have made me sleep in a haunted room.'

'What do you mean?'

'I was attacked,' I replied. 'I was attacked by the ghost of Catherine Linton.' And I told Heathcliff about my dreams.

At first, Heathcliff looked angry. Then he said quietly that I must sleep in his own room for the rest of the night.

I turned to leave the room, but then I looked back. I don't know why. And I saw something very strange.

Heathcliff pulled open the window. He got onto the bed and put his head out of the window. Tears were pouring down his face.

'Cathy, come in! Come in!' he cried. 'Cathy, come to me this time. Cathy, my darling – hear me, please!'

I was very upset. I went downstairs and stayed for the rest of the night in the kitchen.

When I left Wuthering Heights to return to Thrushcross Grange, I was surprised that Heathcliff came with me. The snow was very thick and covered all the roads and paths. Without Heathcliff's help, I would soon have been lost. It took four hours to get back and I was very, very cold when I got home at last.

I put on some dry clothes and sat by the fire in the kitchen drinking some hot coffee. But I felt tired and ill. The moors are bleak and lonely and the people I have met are strange and unfriendly. I came to Yorkshire to be alone, but now I don't want to be alone any longer.

When Mrs Dean, the housekeeper, brought me my evening meal, I asked her to sit with me while I ate it. I hoped that she was a woman who liked to talk.

'Have you lived here a long time?' I asked.

'Eighteen years,' Mrs Dean replied. 'I came here when my mistress[16] married Mr Edgar Linton. And after she died, I stayed here as the housekeeper.'

'This is a much more comfortable house than Wuthering Heights,' I said. 'Why doesn't Mr Heathcliff live here? Why does he rent Thrushcross Grange to a tenant? Isn't he a rich man?'

'He's very rich, sir!' Mrs Dean replied. 'No one knows how much money he has. But he's greedy too – he always wants more money – so he wants the rent a tenant will pay him. It is strange that he is so greedy because he has no family.'

'He had a son who died, didn't he?' I asked. 'And his son was married to the young lady at Wuthering Heights.'

'Yes, that's right,' replied Mrs Dean. 'She is called Catherine. She is the daughter of my dead master, Mr Edgar Linton.'

'So, Thrushcross Grange used to be owned by the Linton family,' I said.

'Yes,' replied Mrs Dean. 'There were Lintons at Thrushcross Grange and Earnshaws at Wuthering Heights.'

'Who is Hareton Earnshaw?' I asked. 'Is he a relation of Mr Heathcliff?'

'No, sir. He is the nephew of my dead mistress. She was called Catherine Earnshaw before she married my master, Mr Linton.'

'Sir,' she went on, 'you have been to Wuthering Heights. Please tell me – how is young Mrs Heathcliff?'

'She looked very well, but I do not think she is very happy,' I replied.

'Oh dear! And what did you think of the master?'

'Mr Heathcliff? He seems to be a very hard, unfriendly man,

16

Mrs Dean.'

'Yes – he's as rough and hard as the stones on the moors,' said Mrs Dean.

'Why is he such a hard man?' I asked. 'Do you know anything about him?'

'I do not know where he was born, who his parents were or how he became rich!' replied Mrs Dean. 'But I do know how he has cheated[17] Hareton Earnshaw, even if the poor young man does not know it himself!'

'Mrs Dean,' I said, 'perhaps you could tell me the story of my neighbours? I do not think I will sleep if I go to bed. I do not feel very well. I think I have a fever. Please sit and talk to me for an hour.'

'Oh certainly, sir,' she replied.

She was pleased that I wanted to be friendly. She brought me a hot drink, then sat down with me by the fire in the kitchen.

PART TWO

3

The Strange Child

Nelly Dean's story

My mother was one of the Earnshaws' servants at Wuthering Heights and I lived there when I was a child. Mr and Mrs Earnshaw had two children – Hindley who was about the same age as me, and Catherine who was eight years younger. We called Catherine, Cathy.

Thirty years ago, in the summer of 1771, when Hindley was fourteen and Cathy was six, their father went away to Liverpool on business.

Mr Earnshaw was gone for three days and when he got home late one night, he brought something strange with him. He brought a child.

Mr Earnshaw carried the child into the house and put it down in front of us. The child was a dirty, black-haired boy.

Mrs Earnshaw was angry with her husband. 'Where did you get that gypsy?' she asked. 'You must send him away.'

But her husband refused. 'I found the child on the streets of Liverpool,' he said. 'He was cold and hungry and no one knew where he came from. I could not leave him there, so I brought him home with me.'

Mr Earnshaw told me to wash the boy, give him some clothes and to put him in the same bedroom as Hindley and Cathy. He said the boy was to be called Heathcliff. No one ever gave the boy a second name.

At first, neither Cathy nor Hindley wanted the boy in their

house. But after a few days, things changed. Hindley began to hate Heathcliff, but Cathy began to like him. She was a wild and mischievous girl and it was difficult to like her. But Heathcliff liked her and became her friend.

I hated Heathcliff too, at first. Hindley and I used to hit him and hurt him as much as we could. But he never cried – perhaps he was used to people treating[18] him badly.

When Mr Earnshaw found out that Hindley was treating Heathcliff badly, he was very angry. From that time onwards, he loved Heathcliff much more than he loved his son.

The children's mother, Mrs Earnshaw, died two years later, in 1773, and soon after that I stopped hating Heathcliff.

In the winter of 1773, all the children were ill and I had to look after them. Cathy and Hindley were miserable and they behaved badly. But Heathcliff, who was much more ill than they were, was quiet and never cried. He was much easier to look after than the other two and I began to like him a little more. And, when the doctor told me that I had saved Heathcliff's life by looking after him so well, I felt pleased. But I knew that Heathcliff wasn't quiet because he was a gentle child. He was quiet because he was hard.

Once, Mr Earnshaw bought two young horses for the boys. Heathcliff immediately took the best horse, but it soon became lame[19].

'You must give me your horse now,' he said to Hindley. 'If you don't, I'll tell your father that you've beaten me three times this week.'

Hindley was much bigger and stronger than Heathcliff, and he picked up a heavy stone to throw at him.

'Go on, throw it!' shouted Heathcliff. 'Then I'll tell your father what you said! You said that you'll throw me out[20] of the house when he's dead.'

Hindley threw the stone. It hit Heathcliff on the chest and knocked him to the ground.

'Take my horse,' shouted Hindley, 'and I hope you fall off and break your neck.'

As he got older, Mr Earnshaw became angry with Hindley more and more often. At last, he decided to send Hindley away to college.

After Hindley went away, Cathy and Heathcliff became closer friends. They were always together – either in the house or on long walks over the moors.

But life was not peaceful. It was Joseph who caused trouble. He was a very religious old man. When he tried to make Cathy and Heathcliff read religious books for many hours, they often behaved badly.

Cathy's behaviour became worse and worse. Sometimes she shouted at me or tried to hit me, even if we were playing a game. She behaved badly to everybody, even Heathclif–but he did not mind what she said or did. He would do anything for her. And she always wanted to be with him. The best way we could punish[21] Cathy was to keep her away from Heathcliff.

In October 1777, Mr Earnshaw died. It was a wild, windy evening. Cathy sat on the floor with her head on her father's knee. Heathcliff lay with his head on Cathy's knee. The old man was touching Cathy's hair gently and she sang to him very quietly. Soon he was asleep, and when Joseph tried to wake him later, he found that his master was dead.

I tried to make the children go to bed, but Cathy wanted to kiss her father before she went to bed. I could not stop her.

'Oh, he's dead, Heathcliff! He's dead!' she cried out.

She and Heathcliff cried and cried, and soon I was crying too. But later that night when I went upstairs to see them, I found that they were very happy together. They were telling each other that heaven was beautiful and that Mr Earnshaw would be happy there. As I listened, I wished that we could all be in such a peaceful place, away from this hard world.

Hindley came home for his father's funeral, and he brought a wife with him! She was called Frances and at first we liked her. Hindley was very much in love with her and he would do anything she asked him to do.

She was a thin young woman with bright eyes. But she had a bad cough. She told me that she was very afraid of dying, but I did not think much about what she said.

Hindley was the master of Wuthering Heights now and he made many changes. He ordered Joseph and me to behave like servants. We had to stay in the kitchen, instead of eating our meals with the family.

When she first came to Wuthering Heights, Frances loved

Cathy. She called Cathy her new sister. She talked to her all the time, kissed her and gave her presents. But then she got tired of her. And when Frances began to dislike Cathy, Hindley began to dislike his sister too.

Then Frances decided that she didn't like Heathcliff, and Hindley quickly remembered how much he hated him. He made Heathcliff live with us in the kitchen, instead of living with the family. Heathcliff had been taught by the minister, but now Hindley ended his education. He made him work on the farm.

At first, Heathcliff did not care that Hindley had stopped his lessons with the minister. Cathy taught him what she learnt in her lessons, and they often ran away to the moors together and stayed away all day. They were growing up as wild as animals. Hindley did not care what they did. He was only interested in his wife.

But Joseph and the minister became angry when Cathy and Heathcliff did not go to church on Sundays. Joseph made Hindley punish them. Heathcliff was often beaten and Cathy was kept away from him. Cathy was very unhappy, but I could not help either of them.

Our lives continued like this. Heathcliff and Cathy became wilder and wilder. They listened to no one. They did whatever they wanted to do. Hindley was often angry, but they did not care.

Then, one Sunday, something happened which changed all our lives for ever.

Cathy and Heathcliff disappeared. When it was time for supper, no one knew where they were. Hindley made me search all over the house and farm. When I couldn't find them, he became so angry that he ordered me to lock all the doors of the house.

'They can stay out all night!' he shouted.

22

It was cold and dark and it was raining. I was worried and opened my bedroom window so I could see them when they returned. After a while, I heard footsteps on the road and saw the light from a lantern. I ran downstairs and opened the door. But only Heathcliff was there.

'Where's Cathy?' I asked quickly.

'She's at Thrushcross Grange,' he said.

'Why did you go there? Hindley will be very angry with you now,' I said. 'He'll throw you out of the house.'

'I don't care about Hindley,' he said. 'Let me in and I'll tell you what happened.'

At that time, Thrushcross Grange belonged to the Linton family. They were a rich family with two children, Edgar and Isabella. The children were nearly the same age as Heathcliff and Cathy. Edgar was fifteen and Isabella was twelve. But the Lintons and the Earnshaws did not know each other well.

While Heathcliff took off his wet clothes, he told me what had happened that night.

'We were out on the moors and we saw the lights at Thrushcross Grange,' he said. 'So we decided to go and see what the Lintons were doing. We wanted to see if Edgar and Isabella Linton are punished by their parents like we are by Hindley and Joseph. We climbed onto a window ledge[22] and looked in through the window of the sitting-room. It was very beautiful, Nelly. It was all white and gold, with red chairs and carpets. Cathy and I could be so happy in a room like that! But Edgar and Isabella weren't happy. They were crying and fighting over a little dog! What stupid children! We laughed and laughed at them.'

'But what happened?' I asked. 'What happened to Cathy?'

'Edgar and Isabella heard us laughing,' he said. 'Then we made horrible noises to frighten them and they called for their parents. Mr Linton sent their dogs out into the garden. We jumped down off the window ledge and tried to run away but

23

Cathy fell and a dog got hold of her foot.

'I got a stone and pushed it into the dog's mouth so I could get Cathy's foot out. Then a servant ran up and found us. He saw that Cathy was a young girl. He picked her up and carried her into the house. I shouted and swore[23] at him and followed them.

' "What's going on?" shouted Mr Linton.

' "It's some robbers, sir," the servant said. "A girl and a dirty, rough gypsy boy."

'Then Edgar recognized[24] us, Nelly.

' "I think it's Catherine Earnshaw, Father," he said. "I've seen her in church sometimes."

'Then Mr Linton remembered me too. "You're that gypsy boy that Mr Earnshaw brought from Liverpool, aren't you?" he said.

'"Father," said Isabella, "look at Miss Earnshaw's foot. It's bleeding very badly."

'So, they decided that Cathy had to stay with them because she was hurt. But they threw me out, Nelly. They wouldn't let me stay with her.

'I went back, and looked in the window again. I was going to smash it and get in and take Cathy home if she wanted to go. But she was happy. She was lying in a chair by the fire wearing clean clothes and there was a white bandage on her foot. Those stupid Linton children were standing looking at her.

'I'm not surprised that they were looking at her, Nelly,' said Heathcliff. 'She is so much better than them, isn't she? Cathy is better than everyone else in the world.'

4

Christmas at Wuthering Heights

Cathy stayed with the Lintons for five weeks. Frances visited her and took her pretty dresses to wear. The Lintons taught her to be a young lady. And when she returned to Wuthering Heights it was hard to recognize her.

She came home for Christmas and as Hindley lifted her down from her horse, he cried, 'Why, Cathy, you are beautiful now!'

The dogs ran to her, but she would not touch them because she did not want to get her new clothes dirty. She gave me a gentle kiss. Then she looked round for Heathcliff.

Heathcliff was hiding behind the settle in the kitchen. I don't think he knew what to do when he saw the beautiful young lady with clean white hands and a fine new dress. Heathcliff was now dirtier than ever. I had made him wash himself once a week but no one else had cared about him while Cathy was away. His skin and clothes were dirty and his black hair was long and untidy.

It was Hindley who found Heathcliff. I think he was pleased to see how unpleasant Heathcliff looked.

'Heathcliff, come and welcome Miss Catherine home like the other servants,' he said.

When Cathy saw Heathcliff, she ran and held him and she kissed him again and again. Then suddenly she stopped and stepped back and started to laugh.

'How funny and dirty and bad-tempered you look!' she said. 'That's because I've been with Edgar and Isabella and they're so clean and tidy. Have you forgotten me, Heathcliff?'

But Heathcliff was ashamed[25] and he was angry and he wouldn't answer.

25

Then suddenly she stepped back and started to laugh.
'Have you forgotten me, Heathcliff?'

'Come now, Heathcliff. You may shake hands with Miss Catherine,' said Hindley.

'Don't laugh at me!' Heathcliff shouted.

'I didn't mean to laugh at you,' said Cathy, 'but you look so strange. If you wash your face and brush your hair, you will look all right. But you are so dirty.'

She looked down at her dress and hands to see if she was dirty too.

'You didn't need to touch me!' Heathcliff shouted. 'I like being dirty! I will be dirty if I want to be dirty!'

Then he ran away.

Hindley and Frances were very pleased. They laughed at what had happened.

The next day was Christmas Day. Hindley had invited Edgar and Isabella Linton to come to Wuthering Heights to have Christmas dinner.

Heathcliff ran away to the moors very early on Christmas Day. He returned after the family had gone to church and he came into the kitchen.

'Nelly, I'm going to be good,' he said suddenly. 'Will you make me clean and tidy, please?'

We talked while I helped him to wash and dress in clean clothes. I tried to make him feel better.

'Don't be jealous[26] of Edgar Linton,' I said. 'You're younger than he is, but you're taller and stronger. You could knock him down whenever you wanted to!'

'I could knock Edgar Linton down twenty times,' he said, 'but he would still be more handsome than me.

'I wish I had blond hair and pale skin, and was dressed in fine clothes. And he's going to be rich one day. I wish I was going to be as rich as him!'

Hindley returned from church bringing the young Lintons with him. He came into the kitchen, followed by Edgar Linton.

27

Hindley was angry to see that Heathcliff was looking clean and tidy.

'What are you doing here?' he shouted. 'Go upstairs and don't come down before it's dark. If I see you again I'll pull your long hair and make it even longer.'

'His hair is so long it must make his head ache,' said Edgar Linton.

Heathcliff forgot about his decision to be good. He picked up a dish of hot apple sauce and threw it at Edgar's face.

Edgar started screaming and crying so Cathy and Isabella came running into the kitchen to see what had happened. Isabella started crying too. She said she wanted to go home. Hindley pulled Heathcliff outside to beat him. I cleaned Edgar's face with a cloth and I whispered to him angrily that I was pleased Heathcliff had thrown the sauce at him. Cathy was angry with him too.

'You should not have spoken to Heathcliff!' she said. 'Be quiet and stop crying!

'And no one's hurt you,' she said to Isabella, 'so you can stop crying too.'

When Hindley came back into the house again he looked cheerful.

'Now – let's have dinner,' he said.

So they all sat down for their Christmas dinner and soon everyone was talking happily. I was feeling sorry for Heathcliff and I thought that Cathy didn't feel sorry at all. But suddenly, I saw that there were tears in her eyes.

Cathy worried about Heathcliff all day. He was locked in his room and she could not go and see him.

In the evening, there was a dance. Downstairs, people were talking and dancing. After a time, I found Cathy upstairs. She was sitting outside Heathcliff's room talking to him through the locked door. No one noticed that she had left the party. Later she climbed out onto the roof and into Heathcliff's room through a small window. Soon, they both climbed out of the window and back into the house. Then I led Heathcliff quietly into the kitchen.

Heathcliff felt sick because of his beating and couldn't eat much. He sat by the fire and stared at the flames without speaking. I asked him what he was thinking about.

'I'm thinking about how to get my revenge[27] on Hindley. I don't care how long I wait. I just hope he doesn't die before I get my revenge!'

'Heathcliff!' I cried. 'God punishes wicked people. We must not punish them. We must learn to forgive people for what they do to us.'

'No,' he said. 'God will not enjoy punishing Hindley as much as I will!'

5

Cathy and Edgar

In the summer of the next year – 1778 – our lives changed again. That June, Frances gave birth to a baby boy. I hoped that everyone living at Wuthering Heights would feel happier now that there was a new baby in the house. But instead there was more sadness. A few months later, in October, Frances died.

Hindley had loved his wife very much, but he did not cry or pray now that Frances was dead. Instead he swore at God and at all of us. And he started to drink. Soon he was drunk most of the time.

He shouted and swore and treated everybody so badly that all the servants left except Joseph and me. No one visited Wuthering Heights any more. The neighbours would not come near the house because of Hindley's drunkenness and terrible behaviour. The minister would not come to the house either.

I now had to look after Hareton, the baby, all the time. Hindley did not want to hear or see his son. As Hareton grew up, I never knew how Hindley was going to treat him. When Hindley was drunk I was worried that he might kill the child.

I remember one terrible day when Hindley arrived home drunk and Hareton started to cry when he saw his father. I was afraid of what Hindley would do so I tried to get hold of the boy. But Hindley picked him up and ran upstairs. He held Hareton up as if he was going to drop him onto the stone floor below. And then, because he was so drunk, he did drop the child!

It was Heathcliff who saved Hareton. He came into the house as Hindley dropped the boy and he caught him before he hit the floor. I know that Heathcliff caught Hareton without thinking what he was doing. I saw the look on his face when he realized that he had saved Hareton's life. Heathcliff wanted revenge on Hindley but instead he had saved the life of his son.

———

I said that none of the neighbours would visit the house. But there was one person who did come – Edgar Linton. Cathy was fifteen now and she was a very beautiful girl. At home she was rude and badly behaved, but she was always polite and gentle when she visited the Lintons. So Edgar began to fall in love with her. He was afraid of Hindley, but he often came to Wuthering Heights when Hindley was not there.

Cathy was pleased that Edgar Linton admired[28] her. But she was still Heathcliff's friend and they were often together when he wasn't working.

Heathcliff had to work on the farm from early in the morning until late at night. He no longer read or studied. He hated Cathy's friendship with the Lintons. He was often angry and bad-tempered. It was as if he wanted people to dislike him. He spoke very little, even when he was with Cathy.

'Why do I spend my time with you?' I heard her say to him one day. 'You don't know anything and you never say anything!'

It was a cruel thing to say and I know that Cathy hurt Heathcliff very much.

On the same day that Cathy had spoken so cruelly to Heathcliff, Edgar came to visit her. Cathy took Edgar into the sitting-room and I went with them.

'Go away, Nelly,' Cathy said to me.

'No. I have my work to do,' I replied. Hindley had told me to stay in the room when Edgar came to visit Cathy.

Cathy knew that Edgar could not see what she was doing, so she pinched[29] my arm very hard.

'Oh!' I cried so that Edgar could hear me. 'Don't pinch me! That's wicked.'

'I didn't do anything!' Cathy shouted.

'What's this, then?' I said, showing the red mark on my arm.

Then little Hareton, who was with me, saw me crying. He began to cry too and said, 'Wicked Aunt Cathy.'

Cathy was so angry that she got hold of Hareton and shook him.

Edgar ran across the room and tried to stop her shaking the little boy. Immediately she turned round and hit Edgar's face as hard as she could.

Edgar looked at her, then turned away and walked towards the door.

'Where are you going?' she asked. 'Don't leave me.'

'You've hit me,' he said. 'You've made me afraid and ashamed of you. I won't come here again.'

I was pleased that Edgar had seen how Cathy often behaved. Now he would understand that she was wild and bad-tempered and he would stay away from her.

I was wrong. He left the house, but he looked back and saw

Cathy standing at the window, crying. When he came back into the sitting-room, they closed the door. Later, I went to tell Edgar to leave because Hindley had returned and was very drunk. When I saw Cathy and Edgar together, I knew that their argument had ended. I knew that they had told each other that they were in love.

When I went back into the kitchen, Heathcliff was there and Hindley had just come in. He had a bottle of brandy in his hand.

'No, don't!' I cried. 'Stop drinking Hindley! Think of your son —'

'Think of him yourself!' Hindley shouted. 'Get out of my way.'

He drank from the bottle and went out of the room, shouting and swearing.

'I wish he would kill himself with drink,' said Heathcliff.

He turned away and I thought that he had gone out to the barn. Later, I found out that he had gone to lie down on a bench by a wall in the kitchen. He was behind the settle and I could not see him. I sat on a chair by the fire with Hareton on my knee.

Cathy came quietly into the kitchen. 'Are you alone, Nelly?' she asked.

'Yes, I am.'

I looked up and saw that she was worried.

There was a long silence and then I saw that Cathy was crying.

'Oh, dear!' she said. 'I'm very unhappy.'

She sat on the floor beside me and looked up at me.

'Nelly, can you keep a secret[30]? Today, Edgar Linton asked me to marry him, and I've given him an answer. Before I tell you my answer, I want to know what you think. Should I marry him or not?'

'How can I know?' I replied.

'Oh, Nelly! I said yes. Tell me if I was right to say yes! Please, Nelly!'

'Well,' I said, 'do you love Edgar?'

'Of course I do.'

'Why do you love him?'

'I love him because he is young and handsome.'

'That is not a very good reason,' I replied.

'And because he loves me.'

'That's a worse reason.'

'I love him because he is going to be rich and I shall be an important woman and live in a very fine house.'

'That's the worst reason of all,' I said. 'But why are you unhappy? Hindley will be happy. Mr and Mrs Linton will be happy. You love Edgar. Edgar loves you. What is wrong?'

'Everything's wrong! Here and here!' She hit her chest and her head. 'I know in my heart and in my soul that I'm wrong! I shouldn't marry Edgar Linton. But Hindley has made Heathcliff into a dirty, rough farmworker. I can never marry Heathcliff now!

'But Nelly, I love Heathcliff– and I don't love him because he is handsome. I love him because we are the same. His soul and mine are the same.'

Before Cathy had stopped speaking, I realized that Heathcliff was still in the room. I saw him get up from the bench and leave silently. He had listened until he heard Cathy say that she could never marry him. Then he left so he did not hear what she said next.

'Hush, Cathy, be quiet,' I said.

'Why?'

'Joseph is coming,' I said. 'I can hear the wheels of his cart on the road. And Heathcliff will be coming too. Maybe he is at the door now.'

'Oh, he could not hear me from the door,' she said. 'He does not know about love, does he, Nelly? He does not know what

33

'Hindley has made Heathcliff into a dirty, rough farmworker. I can never marry Heathcliff now!'

it's like to be in love.'

'Why shouldn't he know? You know. And if he does love you, his life is going to be very miserable when you marry Edgar Linton. He will have no one. And how will you feel when you are apart from him?'

'Apart!' she cried. 'No one is going to keep us apart! No one can keep me apart from Heathcliff. Edgar must learn to like him.

'And Nelly, if I marry Edgar I will be rich. I will be able to help Heathcliff to get away from my brother.'

I was upset to hear her say this.

'Cathy, that is the very worst reason of all for marrying Edgar.'

'It is not. It is the best reason,' she replied. 'Heathcliff is more important to me than anyone or anything else in the world. My love for Edgar is like the leaves on the trees. It will change as time passes. But my love for Heathcliff is like the rocks under the ground. They never change. They are always there. Nelly, I am Heathcliff. He is always, always in my heart and soul. You must never talk of us being apart —'

At that moment, Joseph came in and we stopped talking. I got the supper ready, while Cathy sat by the fire with Hareton on her knee.

'Where's Heathcliff?' said Joseph, looking round for him.

'I'll call him,' I said. 'I think he's in the barn.'

I went out into the farmyard and shouted Heathcliff's name. There was no answer, so I came back into the kitchen.

At last, I told Cathy that Heathcliff had heard part of what she had said. I whispered so Joseph would not hear.

Cathy jumped up, looking terrified, and ran out of the house to search for him. But it was more than three years before any of us saw Heathcliff again.

PART THREE

6

Cathy's Marriage

Lockwood's diary

It is four weeks since I went to Wuthering Heights. How weak and ill I feel.

The doctor says that I must not go out of the house again until the spring. Mrs Dean helps me to pass the time by telling me stories about the Lintons and the Earnshaws – and about my landlord, Mr Heathcliff.

Nelly Dean's story

I was very unhappy about what Cathy had told me that evening in the autumn of 1780. She had not thought about anyone's feelings – Heathcliff's, Edgar's or her own. I felt very sorry for Heathcliff. He had left the room when Cathy said she could never marry him. He had not heard her say that she loved him.

That night, when Cathy realized Heathcliff had disappeared because of what she had said, she became wild with fear. When none of us could find Heathcliff, she went to stand in the farmyard to wait for him to return.

Very soon there was a terrible storm. Thunder crashed and lightning lit up the moors all around the house. The rain beat down and the wind blew strongly. A huge tree branch fell across the roof of the house. But Cathy would not come inside.

When she did come in, it was after midnight. She threw herself down on the settle and would not remove her wet clothes. I could do nothing for her and at last I went to bed.

The next morning, it was sunny when I came downstairs into the kitchen. Hindley was talking to Cathy.

'What's the matter with you?' he was asking. 'Your face is pale. And why are you so wet?'

'I've been in the rain,' she said, 'and I'm cold, that's all.'

'She was out in the storm,' I said. 'And she wouldn't go to bed.'

'She wouldn't go to bed?' Hindley repeated, surprised. 'Why not?'

Neither of us answered. We did not want to tell Hindley about Heathcliff.

But Joseph had come in and heard the conversation. 'She's been running after t'boys as usual!' he said. 'Edgar Linton comes here every time you're away from the house. And when he isn't here she's with that devil, Heathcliff. I've seen her out on the moors at midnight with him!'

'Be quiet, Joseph,' shouted Cathy. 'Edgar Linton was here yesterday, Hindley. But I asked him to leave because I knew you don't like him coming here.'

'You're lying, Cathy,' said Hindley. 'But forget Linton. You were with Heathcliff last night, weren't you? I'm going to throw him out of here today.'

'I never saw Heathcliff last night,' replied Cathy, starting to cry. 'Perhaps you won't have to throw him out. Perhaps he's gone.'

Her crying was terrible to hear. I took her to her bedroom and I will never forget how she behaved. I thought she was going mad. She terrified me with her wild shouting and crying.

The doctor came and said that she was dangerously ill with

a fever. I had to look after Cathy while she was ill. She was bad-tempered and difficult, but at last she began to get well. Mr and Mrs Linton came to visit her and asked her to go and stay with them at Thrushcross Grange. It was sad that they did this because they both caught the fever themselves and died.

Cathy had not changed when she came back to Wuthering Heights. She was as wild and bad-tempered with us all as she always had been.

The doctor was worried that Cathy would become ill again if she got upset or angry. He said that her fits of anger[31] could make her dangerously ill. He asked us to do what she wanted and not to argue with her. We all found it very difficult to live with her, but one person who still liked and admired her was Edgar Linton. In April 1783, he married her and Catherine Earnshaw became Catherine Linton.

Edgar was now a rich young man of twenty-one. He had inherited[32] his parents' property. Cathy was almost eighteen. Edgar said he would pay me well if I went to Thrushcross Grange as Cathy's servant. I did not like Cathy very much and I wanted to look after little Hareton, so I did not want to leave Wuthering Heights. But Hindley told me I had to leave. So, sadly, I left the little boy who I had looked after for five years and went to live at Thrushcross Grange.

At first, Cathy behaved very well. I thought she loved Edgar and his sister, Isabella, very much. But soon I realized that Isabella and Edgar were afraid of Cathy, so they always did what she wanted. And Cathy was pleasant to them as long as they did what she wanted. So Cathy and Edgar were happy together during the first few months of their marriage.

Then the peace of the first few months at the Grange came to an end. It had to end. Strong people like Cathy are selfish. They always make people do what they want. But everybody can be selfish, even weak people like Edgar. When a change came, Edgar was as selfish as Cathy.

The change came one lovely September evening in 1783, five months after the wedding. I was outside, picking apples from a tree. It was getting dark and I could see the moon above the high wall around the garden. As I went back to the house with the apples, I heard a voice.

'Nelly, is that you?'

The moonlight shone on the speaker's face. At first, I saw a tall, well-dressed man with a handsome face and dark hair. Then I saw the eyes. I remembered those eyes. It was Heathcliff!

'I've been waiting here until somebody came,' he said. 'I want to talk to Cathy. Go and tell her that someone from Gimmerton has come to see her.'

'What will she think? What will she do?' I said. I was very surprised and worried.

'Just go and tell her, Nelly!'

I went into the house. When I saw Cathy and Edgar, I did not want to give Cathy the message. They were sitting quietly together, looking at the garden. But I told Cathy that someone from the village wanted to see her.

'I won't be long,' she said as she left the room. 'Please bring us some tea, Nelly.'

'Who is it, Nelly?' asked Edgar.

'It's Heathcliff,' I said unhappily. 'Do you remember him? He used to live with the Earnshaws.'

'What – the gypsy, the farmboy?' he said.

'You will upset your wife if you call him by those names,' I replied.

Soon Cathy came running back into the room.

'Oh, Edgar! Edgar, darling! Heathcliff's come back,' she cried, throwing her arms around his neck happily.

'I never thought he was such a wonderful person,' he replied.

'I know you never liked him,' she said, 'but you must be friends with him now – for me! I want him to have tea with us!'

Edgar was surprised to see what Heathcliff looked like now. He was tall, strong and handsome, his face was the face of an intelligent man and he looked older than Edgar. He looked and behaved like a gentleman. But, when I looked at his eyes, I knew that he was still wild and savage.

Edgar tried to be polite and invited Heathcliff to stay for tea. Heathcliff accepted the invitation. I was worried because I knew that Edgar hated seeing Heathcliff again. When Heathcliff had disappeared, Cathy had nearly died from unhappiness. Now he had returned – a tall, handsome gentleman wearing fine clothes.

Cathy and Heathcliff did not talk to Edgar. They looked only at each other.

'I cannot believe that you are here!' she cried. 'But you've been cruel, Heathcliff. You've been away for three years and you've never thought of me.'

'I've thought more of you than you have thought of me,' he replied. 'I heard that you had got married, Cathy.'

He did not care that Edgar heard what he said.

When at last Heathcliff left, I asked him if he was staying in the village.

'No, Nelly,' he replied, 'I am going to Wuthering Heights. Mr Earnshaw invited me to stay there when I visited him this morning.'

I was worried about what was going to happen now. Hindley hated Heathcliff. Why had he invited him to stay at Wuthering Heights?

'I heard that you had got married, Cathy.'

7

Heathcliff and Isabella

I soon found out why Heathcliff was staying at Wuthering Heights. He had gone there to ask for news of Cathy. Hindley had asked him to come into the house. Several men were there and they were playing cards. Hindley did not have very much money, but in the last few years he had spent a lot of it on gambling.

Heathcliff stayed and played cards with them all day. By the end of the day, Hindley owed Heathcliff a lot of money. Hindley did not have enough money to pay Heathcliff, so he let him stay at Wuthering Heights. Heathcliff was going to get his revenge on Hindley by taking all his money.

It was Cathy who told me all this. Heathcliff had told her how he had played cards with Hindley. She loved Heathcliff, but she knew what kind of man he was. She knew that Heathcliff was cruel. She knew that he wanted revenge on Hindley because of the way Hindley had treated him.

Heathcliff continued to visit Thrushcross Grange and Edgar continued to be unhappy. Soon Edgar had another reason for being unhappy.

For many weeks Isabella Linton was miserable. Cathy thought that she was ill and one day told her to go to bed.

'I'm not ill,' cried Isabella. 'It's your fault, Cathy. You like making me unhappy! You want everyone to love you! You don't want me to be with him. You don't want him to love me!'

'I don't want to believe what you are saying,' said Cathy.

'You must believe me,' said Isabella. 'I love Heathcliff more than you have ever loved Edgar. And Heathcliff will love me if you let him.'

So Isabella, a pretty young lady of eighteen, had fallen in

love with Heathcliff. Cathy knew what kind of man Heathcliff was, and she tried to tell Isabella about him. But Isabella would not listen to Cathy. So Cathy asked me to tell Isabella about him too.

'Tell her what kind of man Heathcliff is, Nelly. He's bleak and cold like the moors. There's no kindness inside him. He could break her into pieces like a bird's egg.'

I tried to make Isabella understand how cruel Heathcliff was. I told her why Heathcliff was still living at Wuthering Heights. He was gambling with Hindley and winning. Hindley had had to borrow money to pay Heathcliff and Heathcliff was taking his money. He was getting his revenge on Hindley by taking all his money. But Isabella would not listen to me either.

———

The next day, Edgar was away from home and Heathcliff came to the house. Isabella was sitting with Cathy when Heathcliff arrived. Cathy immediately told Heathcliff that Isabella was in love with him. Perhaps Cathy was trying to frighten Isabella. Or perhaps she was being cruel.

'Here is somebody who loves you more than I do,' she said, laughing. 'You could be Edgar's brother-in-law, Heathcliff!'

Heathcliff stared and said nothing but Isabella cried out and ran from the room.

'You were not speaking the truth, were you?' said Heathcliff.

'I was,' replied Cathy. 'But don't think of it again.'

Heathcliff was silent for a few minutes. Finally, he said, 'She will inherit her brother's property, won't she?'

'No, she won't. I am going to have lots of sons who will inherit Edgar's property. Leave Isabella alone. You think too much about your neighbours' property and money.'

I knew then that Cathy did not understand how much Heathcliff wanted revenge. He wanted revenge on the people who had harmed him—first Hindley and now Edgar.

———

Three days later, Heathcliff visited the Grange again. Isabella, who had not spoken to Cathy for those three days, was in the garden. I was looking out of the kitchen window. As soon as Heathcliff saw Isabella, he went to talk to her. He had never gone to talk to her before and immediately I was worried. I was right to be worried because in a few minutes Heathcliff was kissing Isabella!

I ran and told Cathy. It was the only thing I could do. She came downstairs with me. When Heathcliff came into the kitchen, she told him to leave Isabella alone.

'Why?' he said savagely. 'I have a right[33] to kiss her if she wants me to. You cannot stop me. I'm not your husband so you have no right to be jealous.'

'Do you like Isabella?' asked Cathy. 'If you like Isabella, then you must marry her.'

'I'll marry Isabella if I want to. I don't have to ask for anyone's permission[34] – either yours or Edgar's.'

Suddenly Heathcliff became very angry. 'You treated me very badly three years ago, Cathy! And you are treating me very badly now! I'll get my revenge.'

'So, I have treated you badly and you'll get your revenge on me!' said Cathy. 'How are you going to do that?'

'Cathy, I don't want revenge on you,' replied Heathcliff more quietly. 'That's not my plan. You are being cruel to me, so leave me alone and let me be cruel to other people. I'll marry Isabella if I want to. But if I thought you wanted me to marry her, I'd kill myself.'

They were angry and silent when I left them and went upstairs to Edgar. I told Edgar what had happened. He was very angry.

'Call two servants for me, Nelly,' Edgar said. 'I'll have him thrown out of the house.'

I ran downstairs and called the servants. Edgar told them to wait outside. Then we quickly went into the kitchen. Cathy and Heathcliff were arguing angrily again.

'You may be happy to let that man shout at you,' said Edgar to Cathy. 'But I won't allow it!'

'Have you been listening outside the door, Edgar?' asked Cathy.

Heathcliff laughed at him.

'You have three minutes to leave my house,' said Edgar. 'If you do not leave, you will be thrown out.'

Edgar looked at me and pointed at the door so I would get the two servants. But Cathy ran to the door, locked it and took the key.

'You must fight Heathcliff on your own, Edgar,' she said.

Edgar ran to her and tried to take the key, but she laughed and threw it into the fire. He fell down onto a chair and put his face in his hands.

'Don't worry, Edgar!' said Cathy. 'Heathcliff won't hurt you.'

'I hope you're pleased with your husband, Cathy,' said Heathcliff, laughing. 'Is he crying or is he going to faint[35] with fear?'

Heathcliff walked across the room and pushed Edgar's chair

with his foot. Suddenly Edgar jumped up and hit Heathcliff's throat with his fist. Heathcliff fell against the wall, coughing. Edgar ran out of the back door into the garden and called the servants.

Cathy made Heathcliff leave quickly though he did not want to go. 'Go away. Go now,' she said. 'He'll be back soon with all the servants.'

Heathcliff broke open the locked door and left the house as Edgar came back with the servants.

Cathy made me go upstairs with her. 'I feel terrible, Nelly,' she said. 'I have done nothing wrong. This is Isabella's fault because she has fallen in love with Heathcliff. And it is Edgar's fault because he hates Heathcliff,' she said.

'I cannot have Heathcliff as my friend and Edgar is mean and jealous. So I'll break both their hearts[36] by breaking my own. You must tell Edgar how upset and angry I am. Edgar knows that it is dangerous to let me get angry. The doctor said I could become very ill if people upset me or make me angry.'

Cathy was very selfish and cruel. She was planning to use her fits of anger to frighten Edgar, so I did not believe that she was going to be very ill.

I did not tell Edgar what Cathy had said about making herself ill. I did not want to frighten him.

Cathy locked the door of her bedroom and would not let me in. She would not eat or drink for three days, but Edgar did not try to talk to her again. He sat in his library reading. He talked once to Isabella. He told her that if she married Heathcliff he would refuse to see her again.

On the evening of the third day, Cathy unlocked her bedroom door. She asked me for some food and water and said that she was dying. I didn't believe what she said about dying. I brought her some tea and some bread.

'What's he doing?' she asked. 'Is he ill? Is he dead?'

'Mr Linton is in the library,' I answered. 'He's reading.'

'Reading!' she cried out. 'Doesn't he know that I am dying? Doesn't he care?'

'Mr Linton does not think that you will make yourself die of hunger,' I replied.

'I don't think Edgar loves me any more,' she cried. 'I don't think you like me, Nelly. How strange! I used to believe that no one could hate me, even though they hated each other. Now everyone is my enemy.'

Cathy became ill with a fever and her behaviour became wild. She had made herself ill. She thought she was a child again. She was frightened of her own face in the mirror. She did not know where she was. When I tried to leave the room to get her husband, she cried out and called me back. She held me tightly.

'Nelly, oh Nelly! I want to be back in my own bedroom at Wuthering Heights.'

She lay quietly on her bed, with tears on her face.

'I wish I was out on the moors. I would be well if I was outside again. Open the window, Nelly. Open it wide!'

Before I could stop her, she got out of bed and opened the window. The wind was bitterly cold. There was no moon and it was very dark. Cathy leant out of the window and began to speak.

'Oh! Look, Heathcliff, there's Wuthering Heights. There's the church and the churchyard too. We've often been there together, haven't we? We've stood beside the graves and called the ghosts to come.

'Will you come to the churchyard now, Heathcliff? If you do come, I'll keep you there. I won't stay there alone. They can bury me twelve feet under the ground, but I won't rest until you are with me!'

Finally, that night, Edgar came to his wife's room. He was angry with me. I told him that I had not known Cathy was ill, but he was still angry with me.

Edgar held Cathy in his arms but at first she did not recognize him. Then she spoke to him. 'So you have come at last, Edgar Linton?'

'Cathy! Cathy, what have you done to yourself?' he cried. 'Am I not important to you any more? Do you love that man, Heath—'

'Hush!' said Cathy. 'Don't say that name! If you say it, I will die now. I will jump out of the window. I don't want you, Edgar. Go back to your books.'

I decided to go to the village and get the doctor. As I walked across the garden I saw something horrible. Isabella's pet dog was hanging by its neck from a hook in the wall. It was tied to the hook by a handkerchief and it was nearly dead. But it began to breathe again when I untied the handkerchief.

Why had anyone done such a cruel thing? I did not know. I hurried on to the village to get the doctor.

When the doctor got to the Grange with me, Cathy was sleeping. The doctor remembered her illness a few years ago. He said she might get well this time if we treated her kindly.

The next morning, we found that there was more trouble. Isabella did not come down from her room for breakfast. Soon a servant came running to us.

'She's gone, she's gone! She's run off with Heathcliff!' the girl cried.

She told us a boy had seen Isabella and Heathcliff together at midnight out on the moors. I ran up to Isabella's room and found that it was true. She had gone.

Edgar would not do anything to get Isabella to come back.

'She went because she wanted to go,' he said. 'I told her I would not see her again if she married Heathcliff.'

48

8

Two Homes on the Moors

We heard nothing from Isabella for two months, then a short letter arrived. The letter was polite and told us that Isabella Linton had married Heathcliff. But at the end of it there was another message. Isabella wrote that she hoped her brother would forgive her. She also wrote that she was sorry she had married Heathcliff. Edgar did not write back to his sister.

Cathy was dangerously ill and Edgar looked after her all the time. In her fever she often said strange and terrible things. She was expecting a child[37] – so there were two lives we wanted to save. Edgar wanted a son who would inherit all his land and property.

Edgar looked after Cathy all winter, but it was the beginning of March before she left her bedroom.

'Cathy,' said Edgar, 'last spring I was waiting to bring you to my house as my wife. Now I wish that you were out on the moors where the sweet-smelling wind is blowing. Then you would soon be well again.'

'I will be out on the moors once more,' she replied, 'but you will leave me there for ever.'

At about that time, Isabella sent me a letter. I still have it, and if I read it now I remember that terrible time.

Dear Nelly,

Last night we came back to Wuthering Heights and I heard about Cathy's illness. I cannot write to her, and Edgar does not want me to write to him, so I'm writing to you.

Is Heathcliff a man or a devil, Nelly? If he is a man, is he mad? I believed that he was a fine man. He told me that I did not understand what kind of man he was. But I did not believe him. He hanged my dog to show me how cruel he was, and I did not say anything. But now I know what kind of man he is. Why did I want to marry him?

This is a terrible place. I am treated like a servant. Joseph and Hareton hate me. I think Hindley is mad. He showed me a gun and a knife which he carries with him always. He told me to lock our bedroom door every night. If the door is ever unlocked he will come in and murder Heathcliff.

Heathcliff hates me. He told me about Cathy's illness and said that my brother had made her ill. He said that he cannot punish Edgar, so he is going to punish me because I am Edgar's sister.

I am so frightened. I hate him, Nelly. I am expecting a child and I am terrified. Oh, I have been stupid! Please come and see me!

Isabella

I showed the letter to Edgar. He said I could go and see Isabella but he did not want to see her.

I did go to Wuthering Heights. It was a terrible place, as Isabella had said in her letter. Isabella looked pale and ill. Her hair was untidy and her dress was dirty. The house was dirty and untidy too.

But Heathcliff looked well and he was dressed in fine clothes. He told me how cruel he was to Isabella. He laughed when he told me that she hated him! And he asked me to arrange a secret meeting[38] for him with Cathy. I tried to refuse, but he would not let me leave the house until I agreed to take a letter to Cathy. He wanted to visit her the next time Edgar was away from home.

I did not give Heathcliff's letter to Cathy for several days. I was frightened of what would happen when she read it. All that time I felt as if Heathcliff was in the garden, waiting. I never saw him, but I am sure that he was there.

At last I gave Cathy the letter, on a Sunday morning after Edgar had gone to church. She sat in her sitting-room by an open window. She was pale and quiet and very beautiful. But she did not seem to be part of this world any more.

Before Cathy had read the letter, Heathcliff came into the room.

'Oh, Cathy! Oh, my darling!' he cried. He bent down and held her tightly in his arms and kissed her. I could see that he knew she was dying.

Cathy looked at him. 'You and Edgar have broken my heart,' she said. 'How long are you going to live after I die?

'I wish I could hold you until we were both dead,' she went on bitterly. 'But, no. You will love other people. You will have children and you will be sorry to leave them when you die. You will not want to be with me in my grave.'

'Don't say such terrible things to me!'

Heathcliff got up and walked away from her to the fireplace. He stood with his back to her.

'Come here again,' she said. 'Don't be angry with me.'

When he did not turn round, she went on, 'Oh, Nelly, this cruel man is not my Heathcliff. I shall love mine and take him with me when I die. He is in my soul.

'Do come to me, Heathcliff!'

She tried to stand up, and at last he turned towards her. Then suddenly she was in his arms again and they were both crying. Heathcliff carried her to the nearest chair and sat down, with his arms around her.

'Why did you leave me? You loved me – you had no right to leave me!' he said angrily. 'But you did. You married Edgar. You should die. You have broken your own heart. And you have broken mine.'

They cried bitterly and kissed wildly.

'Forgive me!' said Cathy.

'I forgive you for what you have done to me,' Heathcliff cried. 'I love the person who is killing me. But how can I forgive you for killing yourself?'

I tried to tell them that Edgar would be home from church

51

'You have broken your own heart. And you
have broken mine.'

very soon. I told Heathcliff he should go.

'No,' cried Cathy. 'Don't go. I am dying – Edgar can't hurt us.'

'Hush, my darling – I'll stay,' he replied. 'If Edgar killed me now, I would be happy.'

Heathcliff still held her tightly in his arms. I could hear Edgar coming up the stairs. I was horrified. What was going to happen?

When Edgar came in and saw them, his face went white with anger and he ran at Heathcliff. But Cathy had fainted and Heathcliff lifted her into Edgar's arms.

'Look after her first,' he said. 'Then speak to me.'

Edgar took hold of her and I told Heathcliff to go.

'I'll come to Wuthering Heights tomorrow and tell you how she is,' I said.

'I won't go back to Wuthering Heights,' he said. 'I'll wait in the garden until you come to me in the morning, Nelly.'

———

At about midnight, Cathy gave birth to a baby girl. Two hours later, Cathy died. She never knew that Heathcliff had gone. She never recognized her husband again.

PART FOUR

9

Terrible Times

Lockwood's diary

The year 1802 has begun, and I am feeling better than I was. How bleak and cold the winter is here! I hope that spring will come soon.

Mrs Dean's story has been interesting. I now understand more about my landlord, Heathcliff. Perhaps I understand why he is such a hard and unfriendly man. I want to hear more about his life. But Mrs Dean does not know how Heathcliff got his money. I wonder what he was doing during the three years he was away. Did he join the army? Did he leave England? Did he become a criminal? I am afraid to ask him!

Nelly Dean's story

The morning after Cathy's death, I went out into the garden to find Heathcliff. He had said he would stay in the garden all night. I had to tell him the terrible news.

When I found him, leaning against a tree in the garden, he looked up and spoke.

'She's dead! You don't have to tell me that. Stop crying, woman! Tell me – how did . . .'

He tried to say her name but he could not. Then at last he spoke again. 'How did she die?'

'She died quietly,' I replied. 'She is peaceful now.'

'How can she lie peacefully!' he shouted. 'Catherine Earnshaw, I hope that you never rest as long as I am living! I hope your ghost haunts me. Do not leave me. I cannot live without you! I cannot live without my soul!'

He cried out like an animal in pain and hit his head against the tree until blood ran down. I felt sorry for him and I did not want to leave him, but he shouted at me to go away.

Cathy's funeral was on a Friday, a few days later. Neither her brother, Hindley, nor Isabella was at the funeral. Cathy's grave was in a quiet corner of the churchyard, near a low wall. Beyond the wall was the short grass of the moors.

That Friday, the sunny spring weather disappeared. It became cold and the wind blew strongly. By evening it was snowing. Edgar Linton shut himself in his room and did not speak to anyone. I sat in the sitting-room with Cathy's baby. It was very late that night when suddenly I heard a noise. Then Isabella ran into the room. She was not wearing a hat or a shawl and snow covered her hair and thin dress. Blood was running down her face from a deep cut.

'I have run all the way from Wuthering Heights,' she said. 'I'll tell you what happened. But first, tell the servants to find me some clothes. And tell them to get the carriage so I can leave here. I cannot stay because Heathcliff might come to look for me. He hates me but he would take me back to Wuthering Heights because he wants to hurt Edgar.'

I made her some tea and put a bandage round her face. She sat by the fire while she told me what had happened.

'Heathcliff was gone from the house all day yesterday. He would not let me go to Cathy's funeral. Hindley was going to go to Cathy's funeral,, but he was too drunk.

'At midnight I was sitting by the fire in the kitchen. Hindley was sitting opposite me. We heard the sound of Heathcliff returning. The kitchen door was locked so he couldn't get in. We heard him walk round to the front door.

"'I'm going to lock him out for five minutes," said Hindley. "Do you mind?"

"'I don't mind if you lock him out all night," I replied.

'Hindley locked the front door and then he picked up his knife and his gun. He was very drunk and I began to become frightened.

' "Lock him out, but don't kill him!" I cried.

'I took hold of Hindley's arm but he pushed me away.

' "I'm going to kill him now," he cried.

'I ran to the window and shouted to Heathcliff.

' "Hindley's got a gun and a knife! He's going to kill you!"

' "Open the door!" Heathcliff shouted at me.

' "Hindley will shoot you if you come in," I shouted back.

'Suddenly the glass in the window broke and I could see Heathcliff. Hindley ran to the window with his knife and gun, but Heathcliff put his arm through the window and got hold of the gun. He pulled it away from Hindley and then the gun went off. No one was shot, but Hindley's knife went into his own arm. He fell onto the floor with blood running from his arm. Heathcliff smashed the rest of the glass and jumped into the kitchen. He began to kick and hit Hindley. I tried to stop him, but he picked up a knife from the table and threw it at me. So I ran away, Nelly.'

Isabella stopped speaking and drank her tea. She stayed for another hour, then she kissed me and left the house. She never came back.

Isabella went to live in London. She and Edgar often wrote letters to each other. In September 1784, six months after she left, Isabella had a baby – a boy. She called him Linton. She wrote that he was a small baby who was not very strong.

Heathcliff spoke to me about the baby one day. When I told him the child's name, he smiled and said, 'So the child is called Linton. They want me to hate him, do they? One day I will have that child, Nelly. I will take him when I want him.'

Six months after Cathy died, Hindley was dead too. The doctor told me that he had died because he drank so much.

Hindley's son, Hareton, inherited nothing from his father. Hindley had mortgaged[39] everything he owned to borrow money for gambling. And it was Heathcliff who had given him the mortgage. Hindley's house and his land now belonged to Heathcliff.

After Hindley's funeral I went to Wuthering Heights. I tried to make Heathcliff let Hareton come to live at Thrushcross Grange. But Heathcliff would not listen. He lifted the child onto the kitchen table and looked at him.

'Now,' he said, 'you are mine. I can treat you the same way as Hindley treated me.'

———

Lockwood's Diary

Now I understand more about the Lintons and the Earnshaws. Hindley had treated Heathcliff badly after the death of old Mr Earnshaw. So now Heathcliff has treated Hindley's son in the same way.

Nelly Dean spoke unhappily about what had happened to Hareton.

'You met Hareton, Mr Lockwood,' she said. 'You have seen that he lives like a servant in his own house. He cannot read or write and he is a rough, dirty farmworker. He does not even understand how Heathcliff has harmed him.'

She still has more of the story to tell me.

10

Young Catherine

Nelly Dean's story

The twelve years after the deaths of Cathy and her brother, Hindley, were the happiest years of my life. Catherine Linton grew up to be a tall, beautiful girl. She had big, dark eyes like her mother, and pale skin and blonde curly hair like her father. She was never wild and bad-tempered like her mother had been, but she was sometimes mischievous.

Edgar was Catherine's teacher and she enjoyed her lessons with her father. She learnt quickly and happily.

Catherine was thirteen before she left Thrushcross Grange and the park by herself. Edgar kept her at home with him so that he could see that she was safe. He never spoke about Wuthering Heights or Heathcliff.

One day, Catherine began to ask about the hills and moors she could see from the windows of Thrushcross Grange.

'When can I walk to the top of those hills?' she asked her father.

'You can go when you are older,' he told her.

The road to the hills ran past Wuthering Heights and Edgar did not want Catherine to go near that house.

Catherine kept asking, 'When can I go to the hills? Am I old enough yet?' And her father always answered, 'No, not yet, my dear.'

In the summer of 1797, when Catherine was thirteen, her father had a sad letter from Isabella in London. She was very ill and she knew that she was dying. She asked her brother to come to London. She wanted to say goodbye to him and she wanted him to take her young son, Linton, back to Thrushcross Grange.

Edgar left for London straight away. He was away for three weeks and Catherine was very unhappy. She often went out alone to ride around the park on her horse.

Then one day, Catherine went out and did not come back at tea time. Two of the dogs had gone out with her. One dog came back but Catherine and the other dog had disappeared. No one could find her. At last, I spoke to a farmworker who had seen her in the morning.

'She made the horse jump over the fence and gallop away towards the hills,' he told me.

I was so worried that I immediately went to look for her. I walked very quickly and soon I saw Wuthering Heights in the distance.

As I came nearer to the farmhouse, I saw Catherine's dog lying outside the front door. I opened the gate and ran to the door and knocked hard on it. The servant, Zillah, opened the door. She had been a servant at Wuthering Heights since Hindley died.

'Oh – you've come for your little girl,' she said. 'Come in. One of our dogs had a fight with her dog and we took her into the house. But don't worry – she's safe.'

'Is your master here?' I asked quickly.

'No, Mr Heathcliff and Joseph are out and they won't be back for another hour,' she replied. 'Come in and sit down.'

Catherine was sitting happily in the kitchen talking to Hareton. He was nineteen now and he was a big, handsome young man. He was staring silently at Catherine.

I was pleased to see Catherine but I was angry with her.

'You're a bad girl,' I said.

'Nelly,' she cried, jumping up and running to me, 'I will have a good story to tell you tonight.'

'You are coming home with me now,' I said. 'If you knew

whose house this is, you would be pleased to go home.'

'It's your father's house, isn't it?' she asked, turning towards Hareton. 'You talked about "our house".'

He didn't answer.

'Is it your master's house?' she asked. 'Are you a servant?'

Hareton began to look angry. I got hold of Catherine and took her out of the house.

'Go and get my horse,' said Catherine to Hareton.

'I won't. I'm not a servant,' he replied angrily.

'You shouldn't speak like that to him,' Zillah said to Catherine. 'Hareton is your cousin.'

'He's not my cousin! He's a farmworker,' said Catherine. 'My cousin is a gentleman's son. My father has gone to get him from London.'

I was angry with Zillah for telling Catherine that Hareton was her cousin. And I was angry with Catherine for saying that her father had gone to get Linton. I made her leave Wuthering Heights as quickly as possible. Now Heathcliff was going to find out that his son was coming to Thrushcross Grange.

———

A letter arrived from Edgar. Isabella was dead and he was bringing young Linton back to Thrushcross Grange with him. Catherine was very pleased that Linton was coming.

'Linton is almost the same age as me,' she said. 'We will be able to play together!'

When Edgar arrived home and brought Linton Heathcliff into the house, the boy was crying. He was pale and thin with blond curly hair. He looked miserable and ill.

'Catherine, you must be kind to your cousin, Linton,' her father said. 'He is not very strong.'

Catherine treated Linton like a baby. She touched his curly hair and kissed him gently and helped him to drink his tea. After the children had gone to bed that night I thought about Linton. I was sure that Heathcliff would make us take his son to

'Catherine, you must be kind to your cousin, Linton,'
her father said. 'He is not very strong.'

Wuthering Heights. What will happen to this weak boy at Wuthering Heights? I asked myself. How long will he live?

Heathcliff did make Linton go to Wuthering Heights. That night, Joseph arrived and spoke to Mr Linton.

'Heathcliff has sent me to get his son,' said the old man. 'I mustn't go back without him.'

Edgar was silent and looked very sad. He had promised his sister he would look after Linton, but Linton was Heathcliff's son. How could Edgar keep the boy?

Edgar answered Joseph quietly, 'Tell your master that his son will come to Wuthering Heights tomorrow. He is weak and ill, and he is asleep now.'

Early the next morning, I woke Linton and told him that I was taking him to stay with his father. He was frightened and it was difficult to make him leave the house. He wanted to stay with his uncle. I felt very sorry for the boy.

We rode to Wuthering Heights and as we arrived Heathcliff saw me.

'Hello, Nelly!' he called. 'I see you have brought me my property. Bring it in! Let me see it!'

Linton was trembling when he got into the house and he started to cry when Heathcliff took hold of him. Heathcliff laughed when he saw the boy's blond curly hair and his thin arms and hands.

'I hope you'll be kind to the boy,' I said. 'He's not very strong and he's the only relation you have.'

'I'll be very kind to him. I'll start being kind now. Joseph!' he called. 'Come here. Take the boy away. Give him some breakfast.

'Yes, Nelly, I will look after my son,' Heathcliff went on. 'I want him to marry Catherine and inherit Thrushcross Grange. So I don't want him to die before Edgar Linton. I want to make sure that I have that land and that property.'

I had to leave Linton at Wuthering Heights and I tried to go away quietly. But as I left, I heard him crying and shouting, 'Don't leave me! I won't stay here! I won't!'

11

Catherine Meets Heathcliff

Time passed and in March 1800 it was Catherine's sixteenth birthday. Her birthday was always an unhappy day for Edgar because his wife had died on the day his daughter was born. Each year, Edgar spent the day alone and went to see Cathy's grave in the churchyard.

The day that Catherine was sixteen was a beautiful day. Catherine and I went for a walk on the moors. We walked on and on, and soon I was tired. Catherine was now a long way in front of me and I saw that she had met two people. When I got closer, I saw that she was talking to Heathcliff. Hareton was standing nearby.

'Who is your father?' I heard Heathcliff saying to her.

'Mr Linton of Thrushcross Grange,' she replied. 'Who are you?' Then she looked towards Hareton. 'I think I have seen him before. Is he your son?'

'Miss Catherine, we must go home,' I said quickly.

'No, that man is not my son,' said Heathcliff. 'But I have got a son and you met him once. You must come back to my house and meet him again.'

I tried to make Catherine go home, but she wanted to go with Heathcliff. Heathcliff took hold of my arm and made me walk with them to Wuthering Heights.

'I want her to see Linton,' he said. 'I want the two cousins to fall in love and get' married. Then, Thrushcross Grange will belong to my son when Edgar Linton dies. And it will belong to me when my son dies.'

When Catherine met Linton she did not recognize him at first. Then she remembered the boy she had met three years before. Linton was taller but he still looked weak and ill. Catherine was very pleased to see him again and talked to him happily. She spoke to Heathcliff.

'You must be my uncle! Why haven't you visited the Grange with Linton? You have lived so close to us all these years and you have never visited us. It is very strange.

'I would like to come here every morning. May I come, Uncle?' she went on. 'And may I bring my father?'

'Your father and I argued many years ago,' replied Heathcliff. 'Come here if you want. But don't tell your father that you are coming. He won't want you to visit this house.'

'Then Linton must visit me at Thrushcross Grange,' said Catherine.

'Oh! I cannot walk as far as Thrushcross Grange. It is four miles away!' said Linton. 'Come and see me here, Catherine.'

Heathcliff looked angrily at Linton. 'Nelly,' he said, 'my son is a weak, selfish, miserable boy. I often wish that Hareton was my son.'

Catherine would not leave Wuthering Heights until late in the afternoon. She and Linton talked to each other and read books. They laughed at Hareton because he couldn't read. I began to dislike Linton because he enjoyed being unkind to Hareton.

The next morning, Catherine told her father about her visit to Wuthering Heights. She asked him why he had never told her where Linton lived.

'I didn't tell you because Mr Heathcliff dislikes me very much. He is an evil man,' Edgar replied. 'I knew that he would be unkind to you because he dislikes me. So I didn't want you to go to Wuthering Heights to see your cousin.'

'But Mr Heathcliff was very kind to me,' said Catherine. 'He said I could visit his house again. He wants me to be Linton's friend.'

Edgar realized that Catherine did not believe that Heathcliff was evil. So he told her how Heathcliff had treated Isabella. He also told her how Heathcliff had become the owner of Wuthering Heights. Catherine sat silently and listened to her father.

'Now you know why I don't want you to go to Wuthering Heights,' said Edgar. 'Don't think any more about Mr Heathcliff and Linton.'

———

Summer came to an end and the autumn began. The weather was soon cold and wet. One day in September, Edgar went for a walk on the moors with Catherine. They both got very wet in the rain and Edgar fell ill. He coughed a lot and soon he was very weak. Then, at the end of October, I fell ill and for three weeks I stayed in bed. Each day, Catherine looked after me as well as her father. In the evenings, she sat alone in the library and read books.

After three weeks I was able to get up, but I was still weak and ill. One evening, I asked Catherine to read a book to me. She read to me for an hour, then she said she had a headache and was going to bed.

Later, I went to her bedroom to see her, but she was not there. She was nowhere in the house. Very late that night, I heard the sound of a horse's hooves outside and soon I saw Catherine. She was climbing very quietly into the house through a window. She did not see me waiting for her.

'Catherine,' I said, 'where have you been? What have you been doing?'

She started to cry and she put her arms around my neck.

'Oh, Nelly,' she said, 'don't be angry with me. Promise you won't be angry and I'll tell you.'

I promised her, but I knew what she was going to tell me. She told me that she had been at Wuthering Heights. She had been there to see Linton every day since I had fallen ill. Before that, she had written letters to him.

Catherine knew that Linton was weak and selfish. But she also knew that he was ill and that his father was cruel to him. She was sorry for Linton and she forgave him when he behaved badly. Linton had told Catherine that he loved her.

'You won't tell my father, will you, Nelly?' she said. 'He will stop me from seeing Linton. You will make Linton and me very unhappy if we cannot see each other.'

I did tell Catherine's father. I decided that I had to tell him. Edgar was upset and worried. He told Catherine that she must never go to Wuthering Heights again.

———

Spring came, the spring of last year, 1801. Edgar Linton was still weak and ill. He worried all the time about Catherine.

'What can I do for my little Catherine?' he said to me. 'I would be happy for her to marry Linton if I thought he would look after her. But I am worried that he is weak and that Heathcliff always tells him what to do. So I must go on making her sad while I am alive. And she will be alone when I die.'

'I will always look after Catherine,' I told him.

In March, Catherine was seventeen. For the first time Edgar did not visit his wife's grave in the churchyard. He was too ill to walk there.

Linton wrote letters to Edgar. He asked for his uncle's permission to meet his cousin, Catherine. Catherine kept asking her father if she could visit Linton. At last, in August, Edgar agreed that they could meet. He said they could meet once a week on the moors near the Grange. He told me that I had to go with Catherine.

It was nearly the end of summer when Catherine and I first went to meet Linton. We rode across the moors until we met him not far from Wuthering Heights. I was horrified when I saw him.

'How pale and thin you are, Linton!' I cried. 'Are you ill?'

'No – no,' he said. 'I'm not ill. But it's hot and I am tired. Let's sit down here.'

Catherine got off her horse and sat down next to him. She talked cheerfully, but she looked upset. Linton had changed. Before, he had often behaved like a selfish, bad-tempered child. Now, he sat very quietly and did not speak to Catherine or answer her questions.

Very soon she said, 'I must go home now, I can see that you don't want to be here with me.'

'No, you mustn't go. You mustn't!' Linton cried, taking hold of her arm. 'Don't leave me, Catherine.'

Linton looked towards Wuthering Heights. 'My father may be coming,' he said quickly. 'Don't tell him that I've been silent and stupid. He'll be angry with me.'

Catherine was sad and disappointed about her meeting with Linton, and she did not want to meet Heathcliff. She pulled her arm away from Linton and got onto her horse.

'I'll meet you here again next week,' she said, and we then started to ride back to Thrushcross Grange.

A week later, Catherine knew that her father was dying. She did not want to leave him, but she had promised to meet Linton.

It was late in the afternoon when we met him at the same place on the moors.

'Why have you come when your father is so ill?' Linton said. 'I thought you wouldn't come.'

Catherine was angry. 'You aren't pleased to see me, are you? Come on, Nelly. Let's go home again.'

But Linton started to cry, then he fell to the ground. He cried and trembled and looked terrified.

'Oh Catherine, you must stay,' he cried. 'I can't tell you

why. I mustn't tell you why. But if you go he will kill me. Dearest Catherine, you love me, don't you? You will say yes, won't you?'

Catherine felt sorry for him. 'Why must I stay?' she asked, gently. 'Why must I say yes?'

Linton cried wildly and kissed her hands, but he could not speak. He trembled with terror.

Suddenly I heard a noise behind us and I looked round. There was Heathcliff walking towards us.

'Hello, Nelly,' he called. Then Heathcliff looked at Linton.

'Get up!' he shouted. 'Take hold of my hand and stand up.'

Linton would not move and Heathcliff turned to Catherine and me. 'You must help the boy,' he said. 'Help him back to the house.'

'I'm sorry,' said Catherine quietly. 'I can't help you, Linton. My father has told me that I mustn't go to Wuthering Heights again.'

Then Linton started to cry even more wildly and held onto Catherine. So, finally, we had to take him back to the house. We did not know why he was so upset and so afraid.

Catherine took Linton into the kitchen and I waited by the door, but Heathcliff pushed me inside the house. 'Come in and have some tea, Nelly. Hareton, Zillah and Joseph have all gone away so I'll make it myself.'

He shut the door behind me and locked it.

Catherine jumped at him and tried to take the key from him. She got hold of his hand and pulled at his fingers but he was too strong for her. Then she tried to bite him. Heathcliff suddenly opened his fingers and dropped the key. He hit her again and again on either side of her head, then he pushed her away from him. I tried to help Catherine but Heathcliff pushed me away too.

'That's what I do to bad-tempered children,' he said to Catherine.

Catherine jumped at him and tried to take the key from him.

He left the room and locked the door again. Catherine ran to me, crying. Linton sat quietly.

'Tell us what your father is doing,' I said to Linton angrily. 'Why has he locked the door? Why is he keeping us here?'

'My father wants Catherine to marry me,' Linton said. 'He knows that her father is going to die soon. And my father thinks that I will die soon too. He wants to be sure that I will inherit Thrushcross Grange when Mr Linton dies. So we are going to be married in the morning.'

I was very angry. 'Are you going to marry Catherine, Linton? You are a silly, bad-tempered little boy! Heathcliff is mad! And you should be beaten for making us come here.'

I got hold of Linton's shoulders and shook him. He started to cough and then he started to cry again.

Just then the door opened and Heathcliff returned. 'So you're crying again, Linton,' he said. 'Go upstairs. Go to bed.'

Linton ran from the room. He was afraid that his father would hit him.

'Mr Heathcliff,' said Catherine, 'let me go home. I promise I will marry Linton. I love Linton and my father will let me marry him. Please let me go home to my father. He will be so miserable and worried about me.'

'Be silent!' shouted Heathcliff. 'I will keep you here. I am pleased that your father will be miserable.'

I tried to make Heathcliff change his mind[40] but he would not listen to me. He took us upstairs to Zillah's bedroom and locked us in. He left us there all night.

The next morning, at seven o'clock, Heathcliff came back. He opened the door and pulled Catherine out. But he pushed me back and locked me in the bedroom again.

I hit the door again and again and shouted, but no one came. Many hours later Hareton brought me a meal, but he would not let me out of the room. I was locked in that room for five nights and four days!

12

The Death of Edgar Linton

On the fifth day Zillah let me out of the bedroom. 'I've been away, Nelly,' she said quickly. 'I didn't know you were here. Mr Heathcliff gave me the key. He said you were here.'

' "Tell Nelly to go back to the Grange," he said to me. "And tell her that Catherine will come back for her father's funeral." '

'Is Edgar Linton dead?' I cried. 'Oh no, Zillah!'

'No, no,' she replied. 'The doctor thinks he will live one more day.'

I ran out of the room and down the stairs. Linton Heathcliff was lying on the settle in the kitchen.

'Where's Catherine?' I asked angrily.

He sat up slowly. 'She's upstairs. She cries all the time but she can't leave. We won't let her leave. She's my wife now.'

'You stupid boy!' I shouted. 'Where is Catherine? Where's Mr Heathcliff?'

'He's outside. He's talking to the doctor who says that my uncle is dying at last. I'm pleased that he is dying because I shall be the owner of Thrushcross Grange. Catherine says it is her house but it isn't hers now. My father says that everything of hers belongs to me.

'She said she would give me her books or her horse if I unlocked the door and let her out. But I told her that she has nothing to give me because everything belongs to me now.'

Then Linton became angry.

'Oh, go away, Nelly. You've made me tired,' he cried. He lay down on the settle again and closed his eyes.

I decided to go to the Grange and bring some servants back to Wuthering Heights to help Catherine.

When I got back to the Grange all the servants were very

pleased to see me. No one knew what had happened to Catherine and me. I went to see Edgar Linton. He was lying in bed with his eyes closed. I touched his hand.

'Catherine?' he said.

'Catherine is coming,' I replied.

He opened his eyes, and I told him what had happened in the past few days. He understood why Heathcliff had made Linton marry Catherine. Heathcliff wanted to make sure that he had everything that belonged to the Lintons – the house and everything else Edgar owned. If Linton died, Heathcliff would own everything.

So Edgar decided to change his will[41.] He decided not to leave his money and property to Catherine. Instead he would ask trustees[42] to look after Catherine's inheritance. Then Heathcliff would never inherit Edgar's money and property.

Edgar sent a servant to the village of Gimmerton to ask his lawyer to come to the house. The servant returned alone. The lawyer had said he was busy, but he would come to the Grange in the morning.

I was going to go to Wuthering Heights next day to get Catherine, but I did not have to go. Late that night Catherine returned to the Grange. She put her arms around me and cried.

'Linton let me out. He hated to hear me cry so much. Oh Nelly! Nelly! Is my father alive?'

'Yes, yes, my dear. Come quietly and you can see him now. But, please Catherine, tell him that you and Linton are going to be happy together. Don't let him worry about you.'

Catherine went to her father. He was very happy to see her and a few hours later he died quietly.

The lawyer arrived soon after Edgar Linton died. He had come from Wuthering Heights. I now found out that he had been paid by Heathcliff to stay away until Edgar died. The lawyer told all the servants except me that they had to leave the Grange.

Catherine and I stayed together at Thrushcross Grange. Edgar Linton was buried in the churchyard next to his wife. The day after the funeral, Heathcliff came to the Grange. He found us in the sitting-room where he had last seen Cathy eighteen years before.

'Get your things, Catherine,' he said. 'I've come to take you home.'

'Why don't you let her live here?' I asked. 'And send Linton here too. You hate them both. You will be pleased if you don't have to see them every day.'

'I am looking for a tenant for Thrushcross Grange,' he answered. 'And I want my children near me. The girl is going to work for me when Linton is dead. I don't want her to live here in this fine house.'

'I will come with you,' said Catherine. 'Linton is the only person I love. I won't let you hurt him.'

'Go and get your things,' shouted Heathcliff.

While Catherine was gone I asked Heathcliff to take me to Wuthering Heights too. But he told me that I must stay at the Grange and be the housekeeper.

He looked around the room and stared at a picture of Cathy. It was on the wall above the fireplace next to a picture of Edgar.

'I will have Cathy's picture at home,' he said. Suddenly he smiled at me. 'Shall I tell you what I did yesterday, Nelly? I went to the churchyard. I told the man who was digging Edgar's grave to take the earth off Cathy's grave. After he had dug out the earth, I could see her coffin. I opened the coffin and looked at her again. Eighteen years have passed but she still looks like she always did, Nelly!'

'You were very wicked, Mr Heathcliff,' I said. 'You should not disturb[43] the dead.'

'I did not disturb anybody, Nelly. Cathy has disturbed me. She has disturbed me all day and all night for eighteen years.

'Shall I tell you what happened the day Cathy was buried?'

he asked. Then he went on speaking before I could answer.

'In the evening I went to the churchyard and I stood by her grave. "I want to hold her in my arms again," I said to myself.

'I got a spade and dug down in the earth until I reached her coffin. Then I pulled the rest of the earth away with my hands. I was going to open the coffin when I heard a sound behind me. It was the sound of someone breathing. I knew suddenly that Cathy's ghost was there. She wasn't under the ground. She was with me.

'I felt happy then. After I put the earth back in the grave, I went home. You may laugh, Nelly, but I was sure that I would find Cathy waiting for me at Wuthering Heights. I thought that I would see her.

'I ran all the way home, but Hindley and Isabella had locked all the doors. I had to get in through a window and Hindley tried to kill me with his knife. I remember hitting him and kicking him, then running upstairs to look for Cathy.

'I ran to her bedroom. I saw where she had carved her name on a shelf. I felt that she was with me. But I could not see her! And for eighteen years Cathy has been with me every day. But in all that time I have never seen her.'

Heathcliff stopped talking and stared at the fire. I didn't speak – I didn't want him to say any more.

Catherine came back into the room and said that she was ready to leave.

'Send me Cathy's picture tomorrow, Nelly,' said Heathcliff.

'Goodbye, Nelly,' said Catherine, kissing me gently. 'Come and see me soon.'

'Nelly won't be seeing you,' said Heathcliff 'I don't want her coming into my house.'

He took hold of Catherine's arm and made her walk out of the house and across the moors to Wuthering Heights.

I went to visit Catherine but Joseph would not let me into the house. I met Zillah sometimes and she told me about what was happening at Wuthering Heights.

Linton was very ill and it was Catherine who looked after him. Heathcliff would not go near Linton and told Zillah not to help Catherine.

One night in October, Catherine woke Zillah and told her to go and get Heathcliff.

'Tell him that his son is dying,' she said. 'Go and get him quickly.'

By the time that Heathcliff came to Linton's room, his son was dead. Catherine would not leave her bedroom for two weeks after Linton's death. Heathcliff went to see her once to show her Linton's will. Linton had left everything he owned to his father. So now Catherine has nothing and Heathcliff owns both Wuthering Heights and Thrushcross Grange.

Hareton tried to make friends with Catherine, but she was unkind and laughed at him. Heathcliff had made him into a rough, dirty farmworker who could not read or write.

So Catherine has no money and no friends. It makes me sad, but I cannot think of any way to help her.

Lockwood's diary

I have now heard the end of Nelly Dean's story. It is the second week in January 1802 and I am now well. Soon I am going to go to Wuthering Heights to see Mr Heathcliff. I don't want to stay here at Thrushcross Grange any longer. I have decided to go to London and I do not think I will return to Thrushcross Grange. I will pay Mr Heathcliff his rent for the rest of the year and tell him to find a new tenant in October. Nothing will make me stay in this wild, bleak place for another winter.

PART FIVE

13

Lockwood Returns to Wuthering Heights

Lockwood's diary

It is September, 1802. Last week I was invited to visit a friend in Yorkshire. I was in Yorkshire on my way to my friend's house when I suddenly decided to go to Thrushcross Grange. I was still the tenant of the house and I decided to stay there for the night.

As I rode towards Thrushcross Grange, I passed the grey stone church and the lonely churchyard. Sheep were eating the grass around the graves. It was a warm, sunny afternoon and the moors looked beautiful. I remembered how wild and bleak they looked in the winter.

I got to the house in the afternoon. There was an old woman sitting outside the kitchen door.

'Where's Mrs Dean?' I asked. 'Is she inside the house?'

'No,' replied the woman. 'She doesn't live here now. She's at Wuthering Heights.'

The new housekeeper was very surprised when I told her that I was Lockwood, the tenant of the house. I told her that I wanted to stay for the night and asked her to prepare a bedroom for me. Then I walked across the moors to Wuthering Heights. Why was Mrs Dean living there?

It was early evening by the time I reached the house. I could see flowers in the garden and the doors and windows were open.

I could hear the sound of voices and through a window I saw a handsome young man sitting at a table. He was reading aloud

76

from a book and behind him, with her hand on his shoulder, stood a beautiful young woman. Catherine Heathcliff and Hareton Earnshaw!

I went round to the back of the house. Mrs Dean was sitting by the kitchen door. I could hear her singing. I could also hear Joseph's voice.

'You should be reading the Bible not singing songs,' he said. 'You're no good and neither is that girl, nor the boy. You'll all go to t'devil.'

Suddenly Mrs Dean saw me.

'Mr Lockwood!' she cried. 'Why didn't you tell me you were coming? Nothing is ready for you at the Grange.'

'Don't worry. The housekeeper is getting a bedroom ready for me,' I said. 'And I'm leaving again tomorrow.

'Now, tell me, Mrs Dean,' I went on, 'why are you here at Wuthering Heights?'

'Zillah left and Mr Heathcliff asked me to come,' she said. 'But, come in, Mr Lockwood. Sit down.'

'Yes,' I said. 'I want to see Mr Heathcliff. I must talk to him about the rent.'

She looked surprised.

'Heathcliff is dead,' she said. 'Hadn't you heard about his death?'

'Heathcliff is dead!' I repeated in surprise. 'When did he die?'

'Three months ago,' she replied. 'Now sit down, sir, and I'll tell you all about it. The young people are going out for a walk, so we can sit and talk. I'll tell you about them and about Heathcliff. His death was very strange.'

Nelly Dean's story

Heathcliff asked me to come back to Wuthering Heights two weeks after you left, Mr Lockwood.

Catherine was lonely and did not have much to do. She argued with Joseph and Hareton wouldn't speak to her. He was always bad-tempered and rough.

'Hareton's just like a dog, Nelly,' she said one day. 'He just eats and sleeps and works and there's nothing in his mind.

'I know why he won't speak, Nelly. He's afraid that I will laugh at him. He began to teach himself to read, but because I laughed he burnt his books. Wasn't he stupid?'

'You were cruel,' I replied.

'Perhaps I was,' she said. 'But I didn't think he would burn his books.'

In the early spring Hareton hurt his arm and could not work on the farm for a while. He used to sit in the kitchen by the fire with Joseph, and Catherine tried to make friends with him.

'Hareton, we are cousins. I want to be friends with you,' she said one day. 'Please, forgive me for laughing at you.'

She held out her hand to Hareton, but he would not shake hands. Then Catherine kissed him gently on his cheek. He still did not say or do anything and Catherine went away. She sat down and wrapped[44] a book in white paper. She wrote *Mr Hareton Earnshaw* on the parcel.

'Here, Nelly,' she said. 'Please give this book to Mr Earnshaw. Tell him that I will teach him to read it. If he doesn't want me to teach him, I will go upstairs and I will never laugh at him again.'

I gave the parcel to Hareton and he quietly began to open it. Catherine went to sit next to him. Hareton stopped looking bad-tempered. He was still afraid to speak to her, but soon I saw them looking at the book together and quietly they started to talk.

*Soon I saw them looking at the book together and quietly
they started to talk.*

They love each other now, Mr Lockwood, and I'm very happy that they do. I will be the happiest woman in England on the day that they get married!

Heathcliff did not speak to us very often during those months. He sat with us at meal times but did not eat much.'

One evening in May, Heathcliff came in while Hareton and Catherine were quietly reading together. They both looked up at the same time and I saw him looking at them.

Both Hareton and Catherine look like Cathy. Perhaps they made Heathcliff think of her. He looked very upset. He quietly told them to go away. I was going to go away too, but he stopped me.

'Stay here, Nelly,' he said. Then, after a few moments he spoke again. 'It is strange, isn't it?' he went on. 'I have worked so hard to get my revenge on two families. I own their houses and now I could get my revenge on a Linton and an Earnshaw. But I don't want revenge now.

'Nelly, there is a change coming. I'm not interested in my life any more – I often don't remember to eat and drink. Sometimes I think I will soon forget to breathe.

'Perhaps you think that I am going mad? But you won't tell people what I am saying, will you?' he went on.

'Hareton always makes me think of Cathy when I see him. Even when I don't see him, I see her everywhere. I see her when I look at the stone floor in the house. I see her in every cloud and in every tree. At night, her face is in the sky above me. Every person I see looks like her. The whole world tells me that she once was alive and that I have lost her!'

'What do you mean when you say that a change is coming, Mr Heathcliff?' I asked. I was afraid. I didn't think he was going mad and I didn't think that he was dying. But I was afraid.

'I don't know,' he answered quietly. 'But I will know when it happens.'

'Are you ill?' I asked.

'No, Nelly. I'm not ill.'

'And you are not afraid of dying?' I asked.

'Afraid of dying? No,' he replied. 'I am strong and well. I will probably live until I am an old man. But I do not want to live. I have only one wish – to be with her. And now I am sure that my wish will soon come true.'

14

Lockwood Hears the End of the Story

For a few days Heathcliff stayed in the house. But he kept away from all of us and spoke to no one. Then, one night, I heard him leave the house after we had all gone to bed. In the morning he still had not returned.

It was April and the weather was warm and sunny. After breakfast I went outside to talk to Hareton. Soon Catherine came to find me.

'Heathcliff's gone into the house,' she said. 'He spoke to me! And he looks so different . . .'

'How?' asked Hareton.

'He looks excited,' she answered. 'He looks wild and happy at the same time.'

I was as surprised as Catherine and I was worried too. I went back into the house. Heathcliff was standing by an open door. His face was pale and he was trembling. There was a strange, happy look in his eyes.

'Will you have some breakfast?' I asked. I wanted to know where he had been, but I was afraid to ask him.

'No, I'm not hungry,' he replied. 'Leave me alone, Nelly.'

He behaved strangely all day. He would not eat and he was

81

restless. He walked around the house. His face was very pale but he was smiling. His body trembled but he was not ill.

He did not leave the house again and at eight o'clock that evening I went to his room. I took him a lighted candle and some supper.

Heathcliff was leaning against the wall by an open window. The fire had gone out and the room was dark. He stood with his back to the window and he was staring in front of him.

'Shall I close the window?' I asked.

Suddenly he moved and I had a terrible fright, Mr Lockwood. That pale face! Those black eyes! He did not look human. I was terrified and I dropped the candle.

He spoke then and his voice sounded the same as it always did.

'Why did you drop the candle, Nelly? Go and get another one.'

I ran from the room and sent Joseph with another candle. I was too afraid to go back myself.

Heathcliff ate no supper and that night he went to a different bedroom. He went to the little room Cathy used to sleep in.

The next morning, Heathcliff was still restless and excited. He sat at the table but would not eat or drink.

'Come, now, you must eat something,' I said.

He did not look at me but he smiled.

'Mr Heathcliff, don't smile like that. Don't stare as if you had seen a ghost!'

'Don't shout, Nelly,' he answered. 'Turn round. Tell me if there is anyone here in the room with us.'

'No, of course there isn't,' I replied. Then I saw that he was staring as if there was something in front of him. He had forgotten that I was there.

Later he went out and he was away from the house all day. It was midnight before he returned. I was worried and afraid and I could not sleep. I could hear him walking restlessly around the house. At last, I went down to the kitchen and started to light the fire.

He came to find me there. 'What time is it, Nelly?'

'It's four o'clock.'

'Four o'clock. I must talk to the lawyer later today. I have not written my will yet. I must decide who is going to inherit my property when I die. I wish that nobody could inherit it. And you must remember, Nelly, where I want to be buried. You must make sure that I am buried next to Cathy.'

'Don't talk like that,' I said. 'You haven't eaten or slept for three days – but you aren't going to die yet. You aren't going to die for a long time. Before you die, you will have time to feel sorry for all the things you have done wrong.'

'I don't feel sorry for anything I have done,' he cried. Then he went away to the little bedroom. In the afternoon he came into the kitchen where Catherine and I were sitting.

'Come and sit with me, Nelly,' he said. 'I don't want to be alone.'

'No, sir, I won't. You're frightening me with the way you're talking and the way you're behaving.'

Then he turned to Catherine. 'Will you come and sit with me?' he asked. 'No, of course you won't. You're afraid of me too.

'Well, there's one who will come and sit with me. She's not afraid. She will never leave me alone. Never.'

He left the kitchen and went back to the little bedroom. Through the whole night and the next morning I heard him shouting and crying out and talking to himself. I sent Hareton to get the doctor. When the doctor came we found that the door to the room was locked. Heathcliff shouted angrily at the doctor and sent him away.

That evening and all night it rained heavily. When I went out into the garden the next morning, I saw that the window of the little bedroom was wide open and the rain was blowing in. I knew that the bed was under the open window.

'He can't be in bed,' I said to myself. 'He must have gone out.'

I found a key to unlock the door and went in to close the window. But Heathcliff had not gone out. He was there. He was lying on his back on the bed. His eyes were open and he looked wild and excited.

I could not believe he was dead. But his face was wet with rain and the rain dripped off the bed onto the floor. One of his hands was on the window ledge. When I put my fingers on it, it was cold. I knew he was dead.

I closed the window. I brushed his thick, black hair. I tried to close his eyes, but I could not. I felt that he was laughing at me.

We buried Heathcliff in the churchyard next to Cathy. Hareton covered the grave with earth, and I hope that Heathcliff is at peace there.

But there are people in the village who say that they have seen his ghost. Joseph says that he has seen both of them Heathcliff and Cathy. He has seen them looking out of that bedroom window every rainy night since Heathcliff died. And a strange thing happened to me a month ago.

I was going to Thrushcross Grange one evening. It was a dark, stormy evening and I could hear thunder. I met a little boy who was crying loudly.

'What's the matter?' I asked him.

'There's Heathcliff and a woman up there,' he said, pointing up the path towards the moors. 'I won't go past them.'

I told him to go home by a different path. I thought he had been frightened by the things people in the village said. But I don't like being out in the dark now and I don't like being on my own in this house. I shall be pleased when we go to Thrushcross Grange.

Lockwood's diary

I was very surprised by this end to Mrs Dean's story.

'You're going back to Thrushcross Grange?' I asked her.

'Yes, as soon as Catherine and Hareton are married. They are to be married on New Year's Day. Joseph will stay at Wuthering Heights and look after the farm,' she said.

At that moment, I heard the sound of the gate opening. Catherine and Hareton were returning from their walk. Suddenly I didn't want to talk to them so I quickly said goodbye to Mrs Dean and left.

I walked back to Thrushcross Grange, stopping at the church. In the churchyard, I found three gravestones near the edge of the moors. The middle grave was Cathy's. Her grave-stone was half-covered by grass. Grass was starting to grow at the bottom of Edgar Linton's gravestone. No grass covered the bare stone of Heathcliff's grave.

I stayed there quietly, watching the insects flying among the flowers. I listened to the gentle wind blowing through the grass. And I thought how peacefully these people must be sleep-ing in this quiet place.

Points for Understanding

1

1 Why has Lockwood gone to live at Thrushcross Grange?
2 Lockwood met Heathcliff for the first time. What does he tell us about Heathcliff?
3 Lockwood went to Wuthering Heights again. Heathcliff told Lockwood he was stupid. Why did he say this?
4 Lockwood met a young man and a young woman.
   (a)   What did he learn about the young man?
   (b)   What did he learn about the young woman?
5 What happened when Lockwood tried to leave?

2

1 Why did Zillah tell Lockwood not to make any noise?
2 What did Lockwood see on the shelf?
3 Lockwood had two dreams. What happened in the second dream?
4 'And I saw something very strange,' says Lockwood. What did he see?
5 Make a list of all the people Nelly Dean talked about to Lockwood.
6 What did Lockwood ask Mrs Dean to do?

3

1 How old were Hindley and Catherine Earnshaw at the beginning of Nelly's story?
2 What did Mr Earnshaw bring back from Liverpool?
3 What happened when Mr Earnshaw bought two young horses for the boys?
4 When did Mr Earnshaw die?
5 Who was Frances? How did she behave towards Cathy?
6 Why did Heathcliff and Cathy look in through the windows of Thrushcross Grange?
7 Why did the Lintons keep Cathy at Thrushcross Grange?

4

1 'But Heathcliff was ashamed and he was angry.' Why was he ashamed and angry?
2 Why did Hindley beat Heathcliff?
3 Heathcliff sat by the fire and stared into the flames. What was he thinking about?

5

1 What happened in June 1778? What happened in October 1778?
2 How did Heathcliff save Hareton's life?
3 Why did Edgar Linton often visit Wuthering Heights?
4 Cathy said something which hurt Heathcliff. What did she say to him?
5 Edgar found out that Cathy was bad-tempered. What did she do?
6 What did Heathcliff hear Cathy telling Nelly?
7 What did Cathy tell Nelly after Heathcliff had gone?

6

1 Why did Cathy become ill?
2 Why did Nelly go to live at Thrushcross Grange?
3 Someone came to Thrushcross Grange in September 1783. Who was he and what did he look like?
4 How did Edgar feel about this visitor?

7

1 How was Heathcliff going to get his revenge on Hindley?
2 'Here is somebody who loves you more than I do,' said Cathy.
   (a) Who was she talking to?
   (b) Who was she talking about?
3 Why was Heathcliff very angry with Cathy?
4 'You have three minutes to leave my house,' said Edgar. What happened before Heathcliff left?
5 Why did Cathy lock herself in her bedroom?

6 Cathy was very ill. Nelly went to get the doctor. What did she see on the way to the village?
7 What news was there the next morning?

8

1 'I will be out on the moors once more,' Cathy said. 'But you will leave me there forever.' What did she mean?
2 Why was Isabella unhappy at Wuthering Heights?
3 'You have broken your own heart and you have broken mine.' What did Heathcliff mean when he said this?
4 What happened that night?

9

1 What happened at Wuthering Heights the night after Cathy's funeral?
2 Where did Isabella go to live after she ran away from Wuthering Heights?
3 What was Isabella's baby called?
4 Why did Heathcliff now own Wuthering Heights?
5 Heathcliff would not let Nelly take Hareton to Thrushcross Grange. Why not?

10

1 Why didn't Edgar let Catherine go to the hills?
2 Why did Edgar go to London?
3 What did Zillah tell Catherine about Hareton?
4 Describe Linton Heathcliff.
5 'Hello, Nelly,' said Heathcliff. 'I see you have brought me my property.' What did he mean?

11

1 How old was Catherine in March 1800?
2 Why did Heathcliff want Catherine to meet Linton again?
3 Why did Catherine go secretly to Wuthering Heights?

4 Why was Nelly horrified when she saw Linton again?
5 Edgar Linton was dying but Catherine went to meet Linton. What happened to Nelly and Catherine. Why?

12

1 'I am pleased that he is dying.' Who was Linton talking about? Why did he say this?
2 What did Edgar Linton try to do before he died? Why didn't he succeed?
3 What happened when Heathcliff went to Cathy's grave after her funeral?
4 'And for eighteen years Cathy has been with me every day.' What did Heathcliff mean?
5 'I have now heard the end of Nelly Dean's story.' Lockwood said.
    (a)   Who died at the end of Nelly's story?
    (b)   Who owned Thrushcross Grange and Wuthering Heights now?
    (c)   Who lived at Wuthering Heights now? What did Lockwood decide to do? Why?

13

1 Why did Lockwood go back to Yorkshire?
2 Lockwood went to see Nelly at Wuthering Heights. What did she say which surprised him?
3 How did Catherine make friends with Hareton?
4 What was Heathcliff's only wish?

14

1 Heathcliff started to behave strangely.
    (a)   What did he look like?   (b)   Where did he go?
2 'Then I saw that he was staring as if there was something in front of him.' What do you think Heathcliff could see?
3 'I found a key to unlock the door and went in to close the window.' What did Nelly find in the small bedroom?
4 Why was Nelly Dean going to live at Thrushcross Grange again?
5 Lockwood visited the churchyard. Whose graves did he see? What did he think about the people buried there?

Glossary

This story takes place in the late eighteenth and early nineteenth centuries. The story is set in the north of England a long way from any big cities or towns. People travel on horses or they walk long distances between houses and villages. There are no telephones and there is no electricity.

Wuthering Heights is about two families – the Lintons and the Earnshaws. The Lintons are very rich and own a big house and lots of land and farms. They have many servants and farmworkers and they are very important people. The Earnshaws are not as rich as the Lintons. But they are not poor– they own a farm and they have some servants and farmworkers.

1   ***park*** (page 6)
    a large area of grass and trees around a big house.
2   ***moors*** (page 6)
    a high flat area of land covered in short grass.
3   ***rented*** – *to rent* (page 6)
    pay money to the owner of a house so you can live there. You are the tenant of a house if you pay rent for it.
4   ***call on (someone)*** – *to call on* (page 6)
    visit. It was polite and correct behaviour for Mr Lockwood the new tenant, to visit the man who owned the house.
5   ***gypsy*** (page 7)
    a member of a race of people who travel from place to place instead of living in houses. Most gypsies are dark-eyed and dark haired. People were often suspicious of gypsies because they were strange people who did not live the same kind of lives as other people.
6   ***settle*** (page 7)
    a wooden seat for two or more people with a high back and arms. Settles were often in the kitchens and living-rooms of farmhouses.
7   ***harm (someone)*** – *to harm* (page 7)
    hurt, injure.
8   ***gentleman*** (page 7)
    a rich man who is important in the place where he lives.
9   ***bleak*** (page 8)
    cold, windy, empty and unfriendly because there are no people.

10   **farmyard** (page 8)
     a large space (often square and with walls around it) outside a
     farmhouse. The farm buildings are usually in the farmyard, eg
     stables where horses are kept and barns where food for the
     animals is kept.
11   **barns** – *t'master behind t'barns* (page 8)
     Joseph speaks in a Yorkshire dialect – a way of speaking in this
     part of England. *t'master* = the owner of the house. *t'missis* = the
     wife of the owner of the house.
12   **realized** – *to realize* (page 10)
     start to understand something.
13   **haunt (someone)** (page 11)
     come back after death to visit someone. Ghosts (= spirits) haunt
     people or places.
14   **sermon** – *minister's sermon* (page 13)
     a minister is a man who is in charge of a Christian church.
     Sermons are religious talks given in church by the minister.
15   **trembling** – *to tremble* (page 15)
     shake because you are cold or afraid.
16   **mistress** (page 16)
     the woman in charge of the house.
17   **cheated** – *to cheat* (page 17)
     do something dishonest or unfair so that you help yourself and
     harm someone else.
18   **treating** – *to treat* (page 19)
     behave in certain way towards someone.
19   **became lame** – *to become lame* (page 19)
     the horse is unable to walk properly because its leg is hurt.
20   **throw me out** – *to throw someone out* (page 19)
     make someone leave somewhere.
21   **punish** (page 21)
     make somebody suffer because they have done something wrong
     or you think they have done something wrong.
22   **window ledge** (page 23)
     the narrow piece of wood or stone that sticks out underneath a
     window on the inside or outside of a house.
23   **swore** – *to swear at someone* (page 24)
     speak very rudely and unpleasantly to someone.
24   **recognized** – *to recognize* (page 24)
     know someone because you have seen them before.

25 **ashamed** – *to be ashamed* (page 25)
feel unhappy or uncomfortable because you think you are not as
good as other people.
26 **jealous** – *to be jealous of someone* (page 27)
feeling angry and unhappy because someone is more clever, richer
or better than you.
27 **revenge** – *to get revenge on someone* (page 29)
harm someone because they have harmed you. If you want
revenge, you want to harm someone who has harmed you.
28 **admired** – *to admire* (page 30)
like someone because of what they look like or what they do.
29 **pinched** – *to pinch* (page 31)
hurt someone by holding their skin tightly between your thumb
and fingers.
30 **keep a secret** (page 32)
tell somebody something that you know. And ask that person not
to tell anybody else.
31 **anger** – *fits of anger* (page 38)
sudden, terrible anger which makes someone behave in a wild
and dangerous way.
32 **inherited** – *to inherit* (page 38)
become the owner of someone's property and money after they
die. A son or daughter had to be an adult (over the age of
twenty-one) before he/she could inherit his/her parents' property
etc.
33 **right** – *have a right* (page 44)
be able to do something without asking someone else if you can
do it.
34 **permission** – *won't ask for anyone's permission* (page 44)
not ask anyone else if you can do something.
35 **faint** (page 45)
fall down suddenly because you are frightened or ill.
36 **hearts** – *break someone's heart* (page 46)
make someone very unhappy.
37 **child** – *expect a child* (page 49)
going to have a baby, to be pregnant.
38 **meeting** – *arrange a secret meeting* (page 50)
plan a meeting which no one else knows about.
39 **mortgaged** – *to mortgage* (page 57)
borrow money from someone and to say to that person they can
take your property if you do not pay back the money.

40 **mind** – *change his mind* (page 70)
    decide to do something different.
41 **will** (page 72)
    a person writes a piece of paper called a will before they die. On
    the will they write the name of the person who will inherit all
    their money and property.
42 **trustees** (page 72)
    people (like lawyers) who will look after Catherine's money for
    her and pay her a small amount of money each year.
        Edgar Linton does not have a son to inherit his property.
    When he dies his daughter, Catherine, will get all his property
    and money.
        At this time, when a woman got married, all her money and all
    her property went to her husband.
        Edgar does not want Catherine to inherit all his money and
    property and then marry Linton Heathcliff. If this happens,
    Linton would then become the owner of everything. Edgar knows
    that Heathcliff would make sure that Linton wrote a will.
    Linton's will would say his father got everything when he died.
    Heathcliff would then get all of Edgar's money and property as
    well as Wuthering Heights.
43 **disturb** (page 73)
    stop someone from resting.
44 **wrapped** – *to wrap* (page 78)
    put paper around something to make it into a parcel.

Exercises

Multiple Choice

Tick the best answer.

1 Why did Mr Lockwood go to Wuthering Heights in November 1801?
a ☐ To write a book about the Earnshaw and Linton families.
b ☐ To rent a house from Hindley Earnshaw.
c ☑ To see the man who owned Thrushcross Grange.
d ☐ To visit Nelly Dean, who had lived there as a child.

2 Who was Nelly Dean?
a ☐ Mr Linton's housekeeper.
b ☐ The housekeeper at Thrushcross Grange.
c ☐ Heathcliff's wife.
d ☐ The mother of Hareton Earnshaw.

3 Why did Mr Lockwood stay for a night at Wuthering Heights?
a ☐ Heathcliff invited him to stay.
b ☐ Catherine wanted someone to talk to.
c ☐ He was waiting for a lawyer to bring a contract.
d ☐ There was a heavy snow storm.

4 Zillah said: 'This is the only bed in the house that no one uses.'
Why did no one use it?
a ☐ Rain often came through the window.
b ☐ It was the bed in which Cathy slept when she was a child.
c ☐ It was next to Heathcliff's room and he disliked noise.
d ☐ There were five rooms and only four people in the house.

5 What happened in the night?
a ☐ Lockwood dreamed a girl came to the window.
b ☐ Lockwood dreamed about Heathcliff.
c ☐ The window broke and Lockwood woke up.
d ☐ Heathcliff told Lockwood to leave the house.

The Earnshaw Family

Complete the gaps. Use each word in the box once.

> son   angry   learn   called   years   master   business   on
> child   family   hated   daughter   returned   brought   wild
> dead   more   part   study   died   work   education   gypsy

The Earnshaw [1]......._family_....... lived at Wuthering Heights on the
Yorkshire Moors. Mr Earnshaw had two children – a [2]................. and a
[3].............................. . In 1771 Hindley was fourteen [4]..............................
old and Catherine was six. Everyone [5].................................... Catherine
'Cathy.' She was already a wild young girl.

Mr Earnshaw went to Liverpool on [5]............................. in the
summer of 1771. When he [6]............................. to Wuthering
Heights he [7]............................. a strange [8]...............................
– a boy aged about seven. 'I found him [9]............................. the
streets,' said Mr Earnshaw. 'He does not know his mother and father. I
could not leave him. He will be [10].................................... of our family.'

Heathcliff was a [11]................................. young boy. He had dark hair
and looked like a [12]............................. . Cathy liked him very
much and they went out on the moors together. Hindley
[13].................................... him. 'When my father is [14].................................,
I will throw you out of this house,' he said to Heathcliff.

Mr Earnshaw began to like Heathcliff [15].. than
his own son. He became more and more [16].. with
Hindley and sent him away to [17]............................. at college.
However, he [18]............................. suddenly in October 1777
and Hindley returned.

Hindley was [19]............................. of Wuthering Heights. He told
Heathcliff to [20]............................. on the farm. Also he ended
Heathcliff's [22]........................... so he could not [23]............................... to
read and write.

96

People in the Story

1 Where did these people live in 1778 – at Wuthering Heights or Thrushcross Grange? Complete the table.

> Isabella   Joseph   Cathy   Edgar   Frances
> Nelly Dean   Heathcliff   Hindley

Wuthering Heights	Thrushcross Grange

2 Who married whom? Circle the correct answer.

a Cathy married Heathcliff / Edgar.

b Hindley married Isabella / Frances.

c Heathcliff married Isabella / Cathy.

3 Who were the parents of these children? Complete the gaps.

a Hareton's parents were ....

b Catherine's parents were ....

c Linton's parents were ....

Mr Lockwood's Diary

Look at the notes from Mr Lockwood's diary. Write full sentences.

1 28 Nov 01: arrived Thrushcross Grange; old house
  28th November 1801: I arrived at Thrushcross Grange, which is an old house.

2 housekeeper Thrushcross Grange Nelly Dean

....

....

3 owner of house Mr Heathcliff lives 4 miles away

....

....

4 walked to Wuthering Heights – a dark and uncomfortable house

....

....

5 snowed; had to stay at WH

....

6 30 Nov 01: talked to Mrs Dean: who is Heathcliff?

....

....

7 Mrs D – old Mr Earnshaw found H in Liverpool

....

....

8 now However of both WH and TG

....

....

Making Sentences

Write questions for the answers.

1 *Who was living at Wuthering Heights when Heathcliff returned?*
   When Heathcliff returned, Hindley was living at Wuthering
   Heights with his little boy Hareton.

2 *How* ....

Hindley spent his time drinking and gambling.

3 *How much* ....

He had lost a great deal of money.

4 *Why* ....

....

Hindley invited Heathcliff into the house because he owed
Heathcliff money.

5 *Who* ....

Isabella fell in love with Heathcliff.

6 *Why* ....

Cathy became ill because she did not eat or drink for three days.

7 *Who* ....

Heathcliff hanged Isabella's dog.

8 *Why* ....

Heathcliff was cruel to Isabella because she was Edgar's sister.

9 *Where* ....

....

Heathcliff waited in the garden while Cathy was dying.

10 *Did* ....

Yes, Heathcliff and Isabella had a son called Linton.

Comprehension

Answer the questions.

1 Why did Hindley die?

....

2 How long did Edgar Linton live after Cathy's death?

....

3 What was the name of Edgar Linton's daughter?

....

4 Who did Edgar leave his money and property to in his will?

....

5 Who did Heathcliff want his son Linton to marry?

....

6 Why did Edgar want to change his will?

....

....

7 How did Heathcliff prevent Edgar from changing his will?

....

8 Who became the owner of Thrushcross Grange when Edgar died?

....

9 Where did Catherine go to live after her father's death?

....

Multiple Choice 2

Tick the best answer.

1 What did Heathcliff do with Thrushcross Grange after Edgar's death?
a ☑ He rented it out.
b ☐ He sold it.
c ☐ He moved there with Catherine and Hareton.
d ☐ He gave it to Nelly Dean.

2   What did Heathcliff ask Nelly to send from Thrushcross Grange the
    day after Edgar's funeral?
a   ☐ A picture of Edgar.
b   ☐ A picture of Cathy.
c   ☐ Some books for Hareton.
d   ☐ Some more things for Catherine.

3   What did Heathcliff do at the churchyard on the day of Edgar's
    funeral?
a   ☐ He dug up Edgar's grave.
b   ☐ He looked for Cathy's ghost.
c   ☐ He held Cathy in his arms.
d   ☐ He opened Cathy's coffin and looked at her.

4   How did Nelly find out about life at Wuthering Heights after
    Catherine moved there?
a   ☐ She visited Catherine every day.
b   ☐ Joseph told her what was happening.
c   ☐ Zillah told her what was happening.
d   ☐ Catherine wrote to her every week.

5   Who looked after Linton when he was dying?
a   ☐ Catherine.
b   ☐ Catherine and Zillah.
c   ☐ Heathcliff.
d   ☐ Nelly.

6   Linton made a will. Who did he leave all his property to?
a   ☐ His wife Catherine.
b   ☐ His father Heathcliff.
c   ☐ His mother Isabella.
d   ☐ It was divided evenly between his wife, father and mother.

7   What did Heathcliff do to Hareton?
a   ☐ He turned him into a fine gentleman.
b   ☐ He taught him to read and write.
c   ☐ He made him a servant.
d   ☐ He turned him into a rough, dirty farmworker.

8 Why did Nelly Dean move back to Wuthering Heights in 1802?

a ☐ Heathcliff asked her to go there.

b ☐ Thrushcross Grange burned down.

c ☐ Hareton asked her to go there.

d ☐ She didn't like living at Thrushcross Grange.

9 What happened after Catherine gave Hareton a book in a parcel?

a ☐ He threw it in the fire.

b ☐ She laughed at him when he tried to read it.

c ☐ They fell in love.

d ☐ They never talked to each other again.

10 Who did Hareton remind Heathcliff of?

a ☐ Cathy.

b ☐ Hindley.

c ☐ Frances.

d ☐ Mr and Mrs Earnshaw.

11 How did Heathcliff behave in his last few days?

a ☐ He stopped eating and sleeping.

b ☐ He refused to get out of bed.

c ☐ He felt sorry for everything he had done.

d ☐ He was suddenly very kind to Catherine and Hareton.

12 Where did Heathcliff want to be buried?

a ☐ On his own on the moor.

b ☐ Near to the home of his wife Isabella.

c ☐ Next to Cathy's grave.

d ☐ Next to Mr Earnshaw's grave.

13 Where did Nelly Dean find Heathcliff's body?

a ☐ On the moor.

b ☐ In the kitchen.

c ☐ In Cathy's room.

d ☐ In the garden.

14 Nelly met a little boy on her way to Thrushcross Grange one evening. Why was he crying?

a ☐ Because he was frightened of the thunder.

b ☐ Because he was lost.

c ☐ Because he said he had seen Heathcliff with a woman.

d ☐ Because he was frightened of the dark.

15 What happened to Catherine and Hareton?

a ☐ They left Wuthering Heights and never saw one another again.

b ☐ They inherited nothing and looked after the farm at Wuthering Heights.

c ☐ They blamed themselves for the death of Heathcliff and were unhappy.

d ☐ They married and moved to Thrushcross Grange.

Macmillan Education
The Macmillan Building
4 Crinan Street
London N1 9XW
A division of Macmillan Publishers Limited
Companies and representatives throughout the world

ISBN 978–0–230–03525–6
ISBN 978–1–4050–7709–5 (with CD edition)

This retold version by F.H. Cornish for Macmillan Readers
First published 1995
Text © F.H. Cornish 1995, 2002, 2005
Design and illustration © Macmillan Publishers Limited 2002, 2005

This edition first published 2005

All rights reserved; no part of this publication may be reproduced,
stored in a retrieval system, transmitted in any form, or by any means,
electronic, mechanical, photocopying, recording, or otherwise, without
the prior written permission of the publishers.

Illustrated by Victor Ambrus
Original cover template design by Jackie Hill
Cover illustration by Darren Diss

Printed in Thailand

with CD edition
2018 2017 2016
18 17 16 15 14

without CD edition
2014 2013 2012
8 7 6 5 4